By

Amber Schamel

Luke 2:7

And she brought forth her first born son and wrapped him in swaddling clothes and laid him in a manger, for there was no room for them in the inn.

And this shall be a sign unto you, you shall find the babe wrapped in swaddling clothes and lying in a manger.

Dedication

The Swaddling Clothes is dedicated to Benaiah Joshua Gideon Schamel, my seventh brother and twelfth-born sibling. He entered this world shortly after the release of the first edition of this book.

Acknowledgements

First of all, I would like to thank my Lord and Savior, Jesus Christ. He is the one that made this possible, and I have seen His hand at work every step of the way. The only thing that's good in me is Jesus.

I would also like the thank my family. My dad, my mom, my 11 siblings, and all of my family who have been so supportive and understanding through this process. My parents have provided mentorship and guidance through this process which has been priceless. My mom is my Brainstorming Buddy and helps me hash out my stories before they go on the page. She is a big part of the story formation.

My critique partners, Sharron & Kristen Martell, my mom, and so many others have helped make this story into what it is. I am so thankful for each of these individuals! The wonderful ladies at Seekerville, the members of ACFW and the other authors have taught me so much! I cannot thank them enough for the investment that they've made into my life and writing.

But most of all, a HUGE THANK YOU to all of my friends and readers! This project would be impossible without your support! Thank you for caring, reading, sharing, and your encouraging words. The fact that you would take time out of your day to read my work or send me a comment is such an honor for me. By sharing these stories with your friends, you have given me the greatest compliment possible.

THANK YOU!

Author's Note

I am so excited for you to join me in the adventure of The Swaddling Clothes! Before we get started, there are a couple things I would like you to know.

First, I have included a Glossary & Pronunciation Guide at the back of this book. This glossary contains Hebrew words and names along with a definition and pronunciation for your reading pleasure. I have also included Scripture references to each of the characters. If at any time you run across a word you do not understand, a character you do not recognize, or a name you can't pronounce, just flip to the glossary to find out.

Second, this is a work of Biblical Fiction, meaning that it is based on actual Biblical events, however I have taken the liberty of expounding on the events found in Scripture. To help you decipher which events are found in the

Biblical text, versus what is fiction, I have included **footnotes at the bottom of the pages** with the references to the portion of Scripture that is included in the story. It is my hope that this story will inspire you to go back and study the Biblical account for yourself.

Again, thank you so much for joining me in this adventure! My prayer is that it will be a great blessing to you, and bring the Bible to life in a way you've never experienced before.

Wishing you a very Merry Christmas filled with love, laughter and blessings as you celebrate the true meaning of CHRIST-mas.

If you don't already know me, I would love to meet you! Here's where you can find me:

Facebook: www.facebook.com/AuthorAmberSchamel

Twitter: @AmberSchamel

Pintrest: www.pintrest.com/AmberDSchamel

or on www.AmberSchamel.com

Part One

Chapter One

Circa 980 B.C.

King David drummed his fingers on the arm of his throne. The merchant's monotone voice had been echoing off the cedar walls of the judgment hall for more than an hour. If he whined the words *unfair taxes* one more time...

"So you see, your highness, these taxes are relatively unfair when considering —"

"Enough!" David's irritation boiled over.

The merchant stumbled backward. His scalded pride evidenced by the scarlet flushing of his round face.

Something squeezed in David's chest. The merchant wasn't the sole reason for his foul mood, and didn't deserve to bear the worst of it. "I'm sorry."

He wiped his forehead. Being the king of Israel was not what he'd hoped. He should be leading his army against the Philistines. Instead here he was, in his luxurious palace, listening to the endless and petty complaints. [1]

Ahithophel clapped his hands. "The king has heard enough of your whining for today. Come back later."

David stood and ran his hand through his hair. Loose curls twisted around his fingers. He paced for a few moments before looking up. Amnon, his oldest son, glared over his shoulder as the aide shooed him out of the hall.

"Ahithophel, it's all right. I can…"

"My lord, their prattle is irritating me as well. It can wait until the morrow."

David ducked out the side exit, into the corridor to the private part of the palace. He stopped, inhaling the comforting scent of cedar, and waited for his aide.

Ahithophel slipped through the door and closed it quietly. His expression was tentative when he faced David.

"I am sorry, Ahithophel, but I am not cut of this pattern. I am the type of king who leads armies into battle, who destroys enemies, a king with a sword constantly by

[1] 2 Sam 11:1

my side." He motioned to the warrior's blade hanging from his belt. "I love my people, but I cannot bear sitting here listening to their petty arguments while my army marches."

"My king, you know we can no longer risk you getting killed in some skirmish. Your sons are still young, and you have not yet determined a successor for your throne. If you were to fall in battle, Israel would be left in disarray."

David stepped closer to him and whispered through clenched teeth. "I can't do this. It's hard enough to stay here cooped up like a child, but listening to their trivial prattle day after day is more than I can stand."

Ahithophel gave him a sympathetic smile and laid a hand on his shoulder. "Take the remainder of the day to rest. Walk the gardens with your new wife, eat a good meal, refresh yourself. You'll feel better tomorrow." He smiled again and disappeared down the hall.

Taking a deep breath, David wandered into the garden and wove through the trees and flowerbeds until he neared the fountain surrounded by pomegranate trees. The rich red fruit contrasted with the soft green of the olive leaves. The trickle of the water fountain and the sweet sound of turtledoves cooing soothed his soul. He should have brought his harp, for a psalm was bubbling up within him.

Standing in the midst of all this beauty was one not to be compared to it. With her emerald eyes set in a complexion of pearl, and ringlets of ruby cascading down her back. Bathsheba. He had loved her since the moment he saw her. His heart had sinned for her, bringing the wrath of his righteous God upon them. But although God had taken their baby, He had not denied him Bathsheba. [2]

Stepping beside her, David slid his hand into hers and gave it a tight squeeze.

"A rough day for my king?"

David groaned. "I am tired of being king. Can't I be something else for today?"

Bathsheba turned around. Her green eyes met his, and a smile curved her lips. She lifted his hands and placed them on her belly. "Then be Abba today."

The breath caught in his throat. "You're…"

Her giggle and nod assured him it was so. Wrapping her in a tight embrace, he lifted her off her feet and whirled around in a circle. Finally setting her down, he placed his hands on either side of her face. "Blessed be the Lord God of Israel who has chosen in His great mercy to bless us. The child will be a son, and he will inherit my throne and reign over the house of Israel in peace and prosperity. There will be no one like him in all the world."

[2] 2 Sam 11-12

His wife's eyes sparkled in the light streaming through the trees. "Yes, our son will be a special child."

"When he is born, I will hold a feast a month long. The armies will rest from fighting to celebrate the birth of the prince of the house of David."

A frown contorted his wife's face. "But, if we announce at his birth that he will be your successor, won't it put him in danger?"

David's hands fell to his sides. He hadn't considered that. "You may be right. There must be another way." How could they appoint this child as the successor without endangering him? He could wait to announce it until later, but what if something happened to him in the meantime? No, wouldn't do. They had to come up with some sort of symbol. Something that wouldn't reveal the secret until the proper time. Something almost prophetic.

An idea ignited in his mind. Grasping Bathsheba's hand, he tugged her toward the palace. "Come. We have lots of work to do."

"David, what are you talking about?"

"My son will not be wrapped in ordinary swaddling cloth. No, this prince is unlike any other child and must be treated as such. We will have cloth woven for him on the looms of Egypt, Sheba, Assyria, and every nation on the earth. At his birth, we will wrap him in swaddling clothes so magnificent no one will be able to deny his royalty. At my death, I shall decree that the son who possesses that certain cloth will be my heir. It will evade the danger, yet make it clear who I desire my heir to be. Quickly. We must find Ahithophel and have him gather merchants from every corner of the city."

*****

Maacah pressed her back against an olive trunk. Had she really heard right? All expected this new, young wife of David's would soon be with child, but how could the child of a commoner — a wife acquired through murder and iniquity — possibly be named the successor to the throne above her own son? Absalom was a beautiful child, beloved of all who knew him, third born, and of royal blood. What disgrace and insolence for David to consider this woman's son over Absalom. No, this could never be.

She peeked out from behind the tree as David led Bathsheba toward the palace. "Something must be done. That woman's son will never reign over Absalom."

Her thoughts raced like wild stallions as she darted toward her son's chambers. She didn't know how, but she would blight this plan to usurp Absalom's throne. Starting with the swaddling clothes.

*****

David threw open the door to his aide's chamber. The energy he'd lost when his army marched from Jerusalem without him had returned. It felt good, and he was ready to commence his project.

His eyes swept the room. Across the bearskin rug stood a sturdy table. The man he sought hunched over it. "Ahithophel."

The aide looked up from the scrolls he studied. "Your highness, I didn't expect you back so soon."

"Where are my scribes?"

The man's eyebrow rose. "You dismissed them, sire."

"Yes. Well, I have a very important decree to issue. Summon the scribes at once."

"Begging your pardon, my lord, but isn't this a bit sudden?"

"Of course it's sudden. Isn't everything urgent sudden?" David could no longer hold back the grin spreading across his face. "Summon the scribes, my friend. Then I shall tell you the news."

Clapping his adviser on the back, he again took Bathsheba's hand and strode toward the court.

Ahithophel scrambled after them, barking the order

over his shoulder. "Sire, please, what is this so urgent decree? What news? Is something wrong?"

David faced his friend as the guards opened the court's great doors. "No, my friend, not wrong, but something glorious. Come."

He settled on his throne, motioning Bathsheba to sit beside him. Ahithophel never could abide suspense, and his pained expression amused David.

"My king, I could serve you better if you would enlighten me."

David opened his arms wide and lifted his gaze toward the heavens. "I am going to be an abba. Blessed be the name of the Lord!" His jubilant cry echoed through the corridor.

A puzzled frown crossed Ahithophel's face. Then his eyes drifted to Bathsheba. "Ah, mazel tov. Long life and happiness to the prince and his mother."

Shuffling in the doorway interrupted their conversation. Five scribes tiptoed into the hall, holding their writing instruments close to their chests.

David clapped twice. "It's about time. Take down a decree from the king."

Parchment rustled, and ink sloshed as the scribes scrambled to ready their tools. David extended a stocky finger toward the city as he issued his command. The scribes copied out his words and presented the documents. After David implanted his seal into the wax of each copy, the messenger carried them out of the hall. Horsemen would be waiting to carry the edict to each province of the land. Word would spread quickly, and he wouldn't have to wait long for tradesmen to begin flowing into the city.

*****

Absalom's resolute step carried him swiftly toward the court. His long tresses, curly like his father's, bounced against his broad shoulders. Could what Mother said be the truth? He refused to believe his father would plan to make Bathsheba's child his heir. For twenty years he had worked to become his father's favorite. She must have heard wrong. She did say she was a distance away as they spoke. He rounded the corner and entered the hall adjoining the throne room. A group of scribes stood in his way.

"You go in first. You're the one who has served the king the longest."

"He threw us out moments ago. Now he wants us back?"

Absalom rolled his eyes and brushed past them.

"I am going to be an abba! Blessed be the name of the Lord."

Absalom froze. The words unmistakably shouted in the king's voice. His *father's* voice.

He barely noticed the scribes bumping into him as they scurried through the doorway into the throne room. What could he mean by that? Was he not an abba already? Even with six sons?

Regaining his senses, Absalom peered around the door left ajar in the rush. King David's chest swelled. His finger extended toward where Absalom stood obscured by the door.

"Let it be written and posted throughout every city in the land of Israel: every craftsman skillful in the art of weaving is summoned to the palace in Jerusalem. The king and queen desire to fashion swaddling clothes for the prince of the house of David. The cloths will be of the finest thread, created from the best of every land. The craftsman selected will be paid a royal wage. A decree from David, king of Israel."

Swaddling clothes of the finest? Crafted from every land? Bile rose in Absalom's throat. His mother had been right. His own father was conspiring against his reign, in complete disregard of his heritage. He could not allow this. Something must be done. Something — but what?

Chapter Two

From his mother's casement, Absalom surveyed the palace courtyard. A merchant ambled toward the hall, arms laden. A red fabric overflowed his grasp and dangled at his ankles. Another balanced a full basket. The colorful threads gleamed in the sunlight. Weavers stood in a long line, clinging to samples of their work. The low drum of conversation reverberated up to him.

Exhaling, he turned from the window. "Imah, please stop pacing. You're going to drive me mad. Besides, you're putting wear on an expensive rug."

Maacah lifted her chin. "Perhaps the king of Israel will issue a decree to find me a new one." Her black eyes glimmered, her sarcasm unable to conceal her rage.

Crossing his arms, Absalom pushed away from the

wall and walked toward the table full of bread, cheese, and wine. He poured a goblet full and sipped it. "We must do something about this whole notion of swaddling clothes. That's the first threat. If the people see this done for the child, they will know who the king intends to follow him on the throne. Then a decree at his death would only be a confirmation."

"Yes, and David still holds the favor of the people. They will agree with whomever he chooses."

"The pregnancy is still early. The child may die as the first."

"Absalom, the first child was cursed by Nathan. The man of God's curse brought the death of their son."

"Then perhaps we shall start there. The man of God must despise my father's sin. It should not be hard to persuade him to curse this child as well."

A slow smile spread across Maacah's lips, accentuating the wrinkles around her nose. "Yes. Yes, but we must wait. The child may be a girl. Late in the pregnancy, we will call upon Nathan. First, we sabotage this plan for the swaddling clothes."

Absalom leaned forward, resting his hands on the table. "But how? The people will favor this idea of a proud king making swaddling clothes for his son."

His mother let out a soft snort. "Have you thought of

the cost of such an expenditure? He has offered a royal wage to the weaver and summoned the most expensive threads from all ends of the earth. This is not wise when a country is at war with the Philistines."

Absalom pressed his lips together. "Indeed. But do not fear, Imah. I will warn the people of this error, and they will soon see through this tender pretext."

*****

David had not anticipated the difficulty of the task he took upon himself. Israel boasted far more weavers than he expected. They came from every part of his kingdom in hopes of gaining his favor and the honor of fashioning the prince's swaddling clothes. With Bathsheba enthroned at his side, he'd interviewed at least a dozen candidates since sunup. If his hunger was any indication, it was now long past noon.

Even the cedar doors groaned in complaint as Ahithophel ushered yet another craftsman into the hall. David heaved a sigh. "Where are you from, and what is your name and tribe?"

With a wide sweep of his hand, the stout weaver bowed low. "Natan, son of Eitan of Debir, from the tribe of Judah."

"State your occupation and experience."

"I am the weaver of Debir. I come from a long line of weavers and have done so all my life."

"What sorts of items have you woven?"

"Anything they need, my king."

David squinted. "They?"

The man puffed out his chest. "Yes, my king. I have woven for every nobleman in Debir. Blankets, clothing, yes, even swaddling clothes. Danak of Debir is one of my closest friends and—"

"Next." David stood and crossed to a window. He winced. The tedious line of craftsmen stretched to the far end of the courtyard.

Ahithophel stepped forward and leaned close to him. "Sire, are none of these good enough for you? Sooner or later we'll run out of artisans."

A flicker of hope. "Oh, are we close?"

His aide exhaled, shaking his head.

Turning to look at the merchant, David waved his hand. "This man is too arrogant and selfish. I don't like him. Bring in the next."

The weaver from Debir clamped his mouth shut and strode out of the court. The dark circles around Ahithophel's eyes testified that he too grew weary of this search. Still, it had to be done. This child was special, his swaddling clothes would be special, and someone special would craft them.

David plopped back onto his throne, stroking his beard. "The man to weave my son's cloth must be a descendant of the tribe of Judah, as I am. Bring me only men of the tribe of Judah."

As Ahithophel disappeared into the corridor, David sat back and turned to Bathsheba. "Woman, what have you done to me?"

Her lips parted in a smile as she squeezed his hand. "We'll find someone. El Shaddai will provide."

Ahithophel again appeared. A man, his gaze downcast, followed him. The shadow of a short beard covered his hard jawline, and when he finally dared look up, his eyes seemed soft.

"Your next candidate, my king."

Something familiar about...David sat up straighter, gripping the throne's armrests. "Who are you?"

"I am Nun of the tribe of Judah. I come from the city of Hebron to offer my services to the king and his son."

"What qualifications do you have?"

"None, O king, but what Yahweh has given me. My family has been cunning artisans since they exited Egypt. My father's greatest boast was that our family contributed to the tabernacle in the wilderness by weaving fine linen of scarlet, blue, and purple for the Holy of Holies."

"So you are well skilled in the craft?"

"Rather, well taught, majesty."

"Can you weave different types of threads into one piece?"

"I can, sire."

This was the one. God truly had provided. David stood and stepped from the throne. "You're the man I can trust with this task, Nun of Hebron. Ahithophel, you may dismiss the others. I have found my craftsman."

*****

Absalom slipped out the door into the courtyard. He slowed his pace as he approached the weavers waiting for their turn to appear before the king and queen.

Nonchalant, Absalom. This is nothing against your wit.

Scowls, shifting feet, and crossed arms. Yes, the craftsmen were growing impatient. Just as he'd hoped.

He pasted on his charmer's smile and addressed a man with a gray mop of hair. "Shalom, friend. Have you been waiting long?"

The man glanced in his direction and kept looking toward the door. "Three days."

"That long? What a shame. Surely my father

appreciates the business you are losing by being here, instead of in your shop."

The man grunted as he stretched his neck, craning to see past the crowds. The door to the hall opened.

Ahithophel appeared. He stood on a block beside a lion statue and cupped his hands over his mouth. "The king has determined that the craftsman must be of the tribe of Judah. If you are of that tribe, please stay. The rest of you are dismissed. Thank you for your dedication to your king and country."

Murmurs rose like a cresting wave. Perfect.

Absalom raised his voice above the grumbling crowd. "This is outrageous. To keep so many people here this long and then dismiss them without a chance? I will have to speak to my father about this. It just isn't right. Please accept my apologies for his behavior. The king will be hearing from his advisors."[3]

"Who are you to challenge the king?" A short, plump man stared up at him through beady eyes.

"My dear man, I am not challenging the king. I am Absalom, his son and royal advisor. I do not wish to challenge my father, but to help him."

A tall man with a beard turned his way. "What would you say to those who think the king was foolish to make

[3] 2 Sam 15:1-6

all his sons advisors when they are less than twenty years of age?"[4]

Absalom let out a sarcastic gasp. "How dare you speak against the king?" He chuckled, as did those around him. This was going better than he could have planned. "Now, we all know my father has a heart of gold. However, he does dote upon his children. Perhaps to a fault." He clasped his hands in front of him. "Take this swaddling clothes notion. Such a heartwarming idea, yes? To make a special cloth to wrap the child in. But is it really best for the kingdom? Think of the cost. Is it fair to make the kingdom pay for his paternal whim?"

The tall man rubbed his bearded chin. Several others stepped closer and fastened their eyes on Absalom.

The opportunity I've been waiting for. Absalom took several strides, centering himself amidst the throng. "If I were king, I would never make the nation pay for such things. Such whims would be paid for out of spoils I earned in battle."

The man with the beady eyes spoke again. "King David has won many battles. He has expanded the kingdom of Israel over a hundred miles to the north and to the south. His spoils have earned him a few whims. David has been the salvation of Israel."

[4] 2 Sam 8:18

"Yes, my father has conquered many nations. But who is conquering now? The armies of Israel are encamped against Rabbah-Ammon. But where is our king? Spending the entire treasury on baby clothes. It is time someone speaks the voice of reason to him."[5]

The tall man dropped his hand from his beard. "Then perhaps you are the man to do it, Absalom. In the meantime, I'm going home."

The line in the courtyard diminished until only a few remained near the door. The short man looked up at Absalom, his beady eyes boring into him. "I warn you, Prince Absalom, such speeches could be interpreted as rebellion. The king would not be pleased to hear of conspiracy in his own house." He drew nearer, his voice lowering to almost a growl. "If I were you, I'd watch your back."

The man brushed past him and disappeared.

---

[5] 2 Sam 12:26

Chapter Three

"David, what do you think about this color?"

David dropped the spool in his hand to examine the silk thread Bathsheba held out to him. The brilliant orange hue shone like the sun. The special fiber hailed from the Far East, where they spun it from the threads of caterpillars.

"Exquisite. Nun, what do you think of this?"

The weaver stepped closer and lifted the thread, rubbing it between his thumb and index finger. "The color and quality is very good, but the thread's weight isn't fitting with the others you have chosen." He turned his attention to the seller. "Do you have something a bit thinner?"

With an enthusiastic nod, the merchant rummaged

through his crates. "It's here somewhere. I know it is. One moment, your majesty."

Leaving the merchant to shuffle through his wares, David motioned to his wife. "Let's examine what we have thus far."

Nun walked over to the throne and picked up the basket of selected threads. "We have indigo from Egypt, to signify the great Nile, golden strands from Sheba, purple strands from a craftsman in Jerusalem, jade thread from Philistia, and blue from Babylon. With the orange from Moab, we merely lack scarlet before we have the seven colors of the rainbow as you wished to have."

Bathsheba squeezed David's hand. "I like that idea. The rainbow was God's promise of peace to Noah. I think it makes a beautiful promise for our son as well."

He smiled at his wife, proud that she too appreciated the symbol. "Not only that, my dear, but Joseph's coat of favor consisted of those colors. Nun, how many threads can you weave into one cloth?"

"In general, about three thousand threads comprise a cloth of this size, highness. However, we can repeat the same threads many times."

"Good. Once we have our seven colors, I want those seven colors repeated with threads from every nation on earth."

"Peace, with every nation on earth." Bathsheba rested her head on his shoulder. "David, how perfect."

"Begging your pardon, majesty." Ahithophel cleared his throat. "Your mother is waiting outside. She requests an audience with the king. She says she has brought a gift."

A gift? David's brow lifted with his curiosity. Imah used to bring him gifts in the fields when he was young, and he'd always treasured them. "By all means, show her in."

Ahithophel bowed and retreated from the room. He returned a moment later with David's mother leaning on his arm.

"Imah, how good to see you. You do not come often enough." David embraced her, kissing her wrinkled forehead.

"My son, I am too old to go wandering about. A dutiful son makes time to see his imah."

"If you would come live in the palace, I could care for you better. It would be more comfortable and—"

Nitzevet held up her feeble hand. "No, my son, you have tried to bring me here before, but I do not belong in a palace." She brushed stray wisps of white hair from her face. "I belong at home where memories of your abba comfort me. Besides, your brothers take good care of me."

David suppressed his worry with a smile. She would not be happy here, but her home in Bethlehem was a cave in comparison to what he could provide for her as the king of Israel. His father had inherited the home, and it was a beauty in its time, but now it was old and small. He had hoped after his father's passing, she would consent to live with him, but it had made her more determined to stay in the old house. Instead, he sent stores of food every week, but he still feared for her safety.

"Anyway." She settled into a chair Ahithophel brought for her. "What is this I hear about another son of David?"

Pulling Bathsheba to his side, David wrapped his arm around her shoulder. "The Lord has blessed us, Imah. We are going to have a son."

A sly smile crossed the old woman's features. "A son, eh? How can you be so sure Yahweh hasn't blessed you with a daughter?"

David frowned. "It's going to be a boy."

His mother chuckled. "It's still a bit early to tell." She waved her hand at Bathsheba. "Turn, my dear. Turn."

Bathsheba obeyed, turning sideways so her mother-in-law could view the bump forming in her abdomen.

"Yes, it will be a boy."

David exhaled. His mother's predictions were never

wrong.

"Well then, rumors have reached Bethlehem about swaddling clothes for the child."

"They're true, Imah. We have been working tirelessly with Nun, our master weaver, to select the threads to compose this royal cloth. We have chosen almost all the colors, but we desire to have a thread from every nation on earth woven into it."

"A lofty goal."

David ran his hand through his hair. "Yes, a larger battle than I anticipated, I'm afraid."

"I have brought something I think you'll find a worthy contribution to your project." She lifted the flap of the bag slung over her shoulder and drew out a braided scarlet cord. She held it in a delicate grasp. "Have you seen this before, David?"

Cocking his head to the side, he examined the cord. "I don't remember it."

"Your great-grandfather wore this cord around his waist. But you're probably too young to remember."

David shook his head.

"This cord saved your great-great-grandmother from destruction. She lived in the city of Jericho. Her family struggled to survive in that city because her father was very sickly. Being the eldest, she felt a responsibility to provide for her family until her brothers were old enough to help, but she only had one option — to become a prostitute. When your great-great-grandfather Salmon and his friend went to spy out the city, she hid them upon her roof. In return, she begged them to spare the lives of those in her father's household. When she let the men out of the window, they made her a promise."[6]

She extended the cord. "'This cord, by which you saved us, will also be your salvation,' they said. 'Hang it in your window, and no harm will come to this house.'"

David reached, but stopped, his gaze lifting to his mother's. "This, *this*, is Rahab's cord?"

A soft smile curved her parchment-thin lips. "It is. Rahab passed it to her son, Boaz, who passed it to your grandfather, and then your father. Now, I pass it to you, to use for your son's royal cloth."

He took the cord and cradled it in his hands. Could this truly be what Imah said it was? Had God really preserved it and presented it to him at such a perfect time? "Bathsheba, look." He gaped at it, caressing threads scarcely aged at all. "Scarlet from Jericho. Can you work this in, Nun?"

The weaver stepped forward and examined the cord. "It will be a challenge, but I think if we match the heavier

[6] Joshua 2

weight of these strands, we can make it work."

Nitzevet held up a finger. "I have one thing more."

Again reaching into her bag, she pulled out a pure white cloth of fine linen. "This is the veil Ruth wore the night she laid down at Boaz's feet.[7] She wrapped your grandfather in it when he was born, so of course he kept it. He was quite sentimental."

"Imah…this is amazing. How, by God's mercy, did you find these?"

"They were part of your father's inheritance. When he passed away, I started going through the different trunks and found both of these along with his other keepsake items. When I heard of your new endeavor, I thought of them."

Nun lifted the veil from her hands and inspected it. He looked up at David and raised an eyebrow. "You are testing my skill, majesty."

David clapped him on the back. "You can do it, my friend. The Lord will guide your fingers."

*****

"Mother, I think that man was threatening me. How dare he threaten a son of David?" Absalom slumped against the wall, the warning in the short man's eyes filling his memory.

[7] Ruth 3

His mother pressed her index finger to her temple. "You must be more careful, my son. Some of David's subjects are loyal enough to kill even his most beloved sons to protect him. Perhaps we best change our strategy."

"But what else can we do? It's still too soon to go to the prophet."

"Perhaps now is the time for you to go to your abba and speak to him. It may be that you can convince him to leave this swaddling clothes idea. Remind him of how much he loves and trusts you, of your capability in ruling the kingdom."

Both their heads snapped toward the sound of a knock on the door. Tamar's timid voice came from the other side. "Mother, brother, it is I. Open the door."

The door creaked as Absalom opened it. He smiled at his sister. With her long ringlets of ebony hair bouncing beside sun kissed cheeks and plump lips, it was easy to see why no one denied that she was the most beautiful maiden in the palace. Her slender form and playful eyes had even caught the attention of his half-brother Amnon, who made efforts to woo her.[8] Absalom insisted on accompanying her to any gathering to shield her from the incessant attentions of all the men present. Truly, his

[8] 2 Sam 13:1 Tamar is later raped by her half-brother Amnon. See 2 Sam 13.

father should be more alert in safeguarding her. Of course, he ignored many such important matters.

"Tamar, what have you been doing? Your face is flushed."

Her graceful hand lifted to close the door, and her lips pursed together. She eased onto the sofa across from them, taking seconds to catch her breath. "I just ran into Bathsheba. She was perfectly giddy."

Maacah's brow furrowed. "Why?"

"I'll give you one guess." A slight smile lifted the corners of her mouth. "But I went along with it and let her chatter about all the news. They've selected a weaver, Nun of Hebron. They've been browsing threads from all over the world, and it's worse than we thought. They are weaving in symbols of the child's assent to the throne, the seven colors of the rainbow, with threads from every country under heaven."

"I knew this would happen," Absalom growled, clenching his fists. "These swaddling clothes will be detrimental to us."

"There's more. David's imah visited today. She predicts the child will indeed be a son."

Absalom slammed his fist into the stone wall. "No! Her predictions are never wrong."

"Worse, she has endorsed this swaddling clothes

notion by bringing family keepsakes from David's lineage to incorporate."

"This will make things more difficult." Maacah sighed.

"I will never convince him against this now." Absalom stroked his beard. "You're right, Mother. It's time to change our strategy. What did you say was the name of the weaver?"

Chapter Four

Absalom sniffed the red wine in his goblet before taking a sip. The tart flavor tickled his taste buds, and then burned his throat as he swallowed.

A servant tapped at the door. "Pardon the interruption, my prince. Achbed has arrived."

"Has he? I suppose it took a week for him to find a convenient time in his schedule to answer my summons."

The servant toyed with his rope belt. An annoying habit.

"Show him in." As the servant scurried away, Absalom took the opportunity to refill his cup. He would have to curb his irritation. Achbed was loyal—as far as his greed went—and Absalom could control that.

The door slid open, and the assassin's gigantic form

filled the doorway. Gold chains jingled around his neck as he ambled into the chamber, his heavy steps booming like thunder.

Absalom flung his leg over the arm of the chair as he stared into his goblet. "You're late. I could have hired three others to do the job by now."

Achbed snorted, his voice lower than the city well. "But you haven't."

The goblet now empty, Absalom tossed it aside. It clattered onto the table, red droplets splattering Achbed's sandals. "No, I didn't. I would have, had I not known your ability to keep things quiet and valued it for this job."

A sneer crept across Achbed's face. "You've got something interesting for me this time. What is it?"

"I don't fancy my father's swaddling clothes notion. I've decided I want it stopped. I will need a certain person, shall we say, quietly removed."

"I think you speak of something within my skills."

Absalom held out a strip of paper. Achbed took it and unfolded it. His eyes scanned the lines, and his unibrow buckled. "There's two names here."

"Mozel tov. You can read. The first is the name of the craftsman making the cloth. The second should be pretty self-explanatory."

"This one will cost you more than the others."

Absalom stood and opened a small chest on his table. He tipped the chest of coins so Achbed could see inside. "I think you'll be satisfied with our arrangement."

*****

"Chariots, gold, provisions, horses, more men. Is there anything Joab doesn't want?" David allowed the scroll to roll shut and massaged his temples with his thumbs. The sooner Joab took Rabbah-Ammon, the better.

"It does seem like a lot, especially when considering how the treasury is dwindling these days." Poor Ahithophel. His beard held more gray than it had a couple months ago...and when had he formed wrinkles around his eyes?

David cringed. Handling all the weavers, and then the merchant traffic, negotiating prices and arranging deliveries was wearing on his trusted aide. "You're looking poorly, Ahithophel. I think you need a day of rest. Why don't you—"

A guard burst through the hall doors, his face flushed. "Lord King, Ahithophel! Come quickly!"

David dashed to the door of the court with Ahithophel following. His hand instinctively rested upon the sword slung at his side. He pushed through the heavy cedar doors as several guards gathered around a doubled-over figure. As he drew near, he recognized the body slung across the guard's back. Nun.

He helped lift the weaver's form and lowered him to the cobblestones. "What has happened?"

"I-I found..." The guard paused, panting deeply. "I found him locked in the small room where he keeps his loom. Smoke filled the place, and he lay unconscious on the floor. Some of the fabric and threads had caught on fire. Others were putting it out as I carried him away."

Ahithophel motioned to one of the guards nearby. "Bring the priest and physician. Quickly."

David tapped the weaver's cheeks. "Nun, Nun, wake up."

The man's eyes didn't open. He didn't groan, or even wince. David knelt at his side, then lowered his head and listened for a heartbeat, trying to control the pounding of his own. "He's still alive, but his breathing is very shallow. Bring him inside and lay him on my couch."

By the time they situated him on the cushions, the guard arrived with the physician.

"Back away from the patient, please. We need the windows opened. As much airflow as possible." The physician bent over Nun and examined his nose and throat. Then he peeled back his eyelids and peered at his pupils. He glanced at David. "This doesn't look good, my lord."

Anxious sweat trickled down David's throat. "You have to save this man. Isn't there anything we can do?"

"I'll do what I can, but if you want this man to live, I would recommend you pray."

*****

Whispering a prayer to the Almighty, David paced across the rug covering the floor of his royal chamber. Bathsheba's soft weeping murmured across the room where she sat with a handkerchief held to her nose.

Ahithophel poked his head through the open door. "My lord?"

David rubbed his weary eyes with his fist. "Is he any better?"

The aide sighed and came to stand next to him. "Still unconscious I'm afraid. The physician has been trying all his potions on him, but to no avail."

A low groan emanated from David's throat. "How much of the material was damaged?"

"Several skeins from Persia and Babylon were destroyed, but the rest remained unharmed. I have already ordered the replacements." Ahithophel shifted, gaze skittering.

Why did the man always do that? Was he so fearsome that his closest aide was afraid to speak his mind?

"What is it, Ahithophel?"

"A servant from your brother's household just arrived. He requests audience with you right away."

That couldn't be good. David's brothers always came themselves if the news was pleasant. He followed Ahithophel with quick steps. The servant soon came into view as they entered the courtyard. Tares stuck to the hem of his linen garment, and a jagged rip reached his left knee. Dirt and tears streaked his familiar face, and his chest still heaved from his apparent haste.

"Caleb, what's wrong? Is my brother all right?"

"Not thy brother, my lord. It is thy mother. She has perished, bitten by an adder."

Caleb's words battered David as if a beam had struck him in the chest. And the blow left him reeling. An involuntary whimper escaped his lips. He grabbed the nearest tree to steady himself as the meaning of the servant's tidings sank deep into his gut. Uttering a cry of grief, he tore his clothes, allowed himself to sink to the ground, and threw dust upon his head. Bathsheba began the death wail, and after a few moments, they commenced the sorrowful march to his brother's house in Bethlehem.

Many more joined in the procession as word of the tragedy spread, and soon mourners filled the road between Jerusalem and Bethlehem. When they approached Eliab's dwelling, his brother stood at the gate waiting for him with his arms folded across his broad chest and a hard expression lining his sharp features.

David swallowed and tried to speak. "Tell me Caleb's words are not true. Does our mother still live?"

Without a word, Eliab led David through the courtyard into the house where their mother lay on a plain wooden bed covered by a blanket.

Eliab stepped aside. "This morning she never came out of her chamber. When my wife went to check on her, she was dead. I inspected the body and found the bite of an adder on her arm."

David winced as Eliab lifted the blanket exposing their mother's face. Her fragile features contorted from the painfulness of her death.

His brother pointed to two round punctures near the veins on her arm. "There."

"Oh, Imah." David fingered the wounds as tears blurred his vision. He looked up at his brother who eyed him intently. "What is it?"

"We've not seen adders near here in years. Now one kills Imah?"

"What are you saying?"

Eliab leaned forward, his voice hoarse. "I smell treachery."

"You think our imah was assassinated?"

Crossing his hairy arms over his chest, Eliab nodded. "She is the mother of the king of Israel."

"I see. So her death is my fault."

His brother arched one black eyebrow. "Really, brother, what else makes sense? If you want to hurt the king, you kill his family."

"But…by no means could the Philistines have done this."

"No, I don't think so. Who else would? Think, David."

"I don't know. The last time I saw Imah, she came to congratulate me on the child. She predicted it would be…"

Wait. The child. A boy. An heir. David's heart sunk in his chest.

"A boy. She predicted the child would be a boy. I think you're right, Eliab. Someone didn't like her predictions. Someone concerned about who inherits the throne."

Eliab shifted his feet, shadows deepening his features. "Sounds probable. All your children will assemble, of course, for the ceremonies. If we are watchful, perhaps we can gather some clues."

The thought that one of his own sons might be the murderer was more than David cared to consider. "It is only fitting to have the ceremony here. She and Abba both loved Bethlehem."

"Yes, she might rise from the dead and switch us if we had it anywhere else."

David surveyed the dwelling. "The courtyard here is too small to accommodate as many as will gather."

"The family will fit inside. Everyone else will have to overflow into the street."

"Considering the circumstances, let's put the funeral off until tomorrow. That will give no excuse for the absence of any of my children."

"Very well then. Tomorrow, but before noon. Imah wouldn't want to stretch the grace of the law."

David glanced again at Imah's form on the bed. He choked, covered his mouth with both hands, and ducked out of the chamber. There was something morbid in breathing the scent of his mother's corpse. That was more than even his warrior heart could take. He braced against the stone wall and wept.

*****

The next morning, nary a tear remained for David to

cry. The hint of sunrise crested the horizon as he made his way out of the palace toward Bethlehem. Grit clung to his cheeks while he tramped along the dirt road. A hand slipped into his, and his gaze met Bathsheba's. Her soft jade eyes gleamed with sorrow and compassion, somehow infusing strength into his worn body.

He paused and planted a kiss on her fair hand. "You didn't have to come with me. You could have come later."

"Where you go, I will go."

Without releasing her hand, he continued down the street. How much should he tell her? He didn't wish to burden her or cause her to fret more than she should. Especially with the babe coming along. "I want to be the first to arrive."

"An honor your imah would appreciate."

He smiled at her, hoping his eyes didn't betray his thoughts. Arriving first so he could keep a watchful eye on each of his children — looking for signs of a murderer — wasn't what he considered an honor to his mother. Quite the opposite.

The long walk in the early morning air failed to refresh his senses. The chirping of the birds, the freshness of the breeze, even Bathsheba's hand in his could not make his worries disappear. Rather, the familiar sight of the courtyard drove them like a wedge with heavy force deeper into the creases of his heart and mind. A large stone already propped the gate open. David remembered running through the gate countless times, dodging the honeybees from the hollow of the old sycamore in the corner. His imah would click her tongue and shake her head at his relentless efforts to extract honeycomb. Blinking away the memory, he noticed his brother's tall form hunched over the fire pit at the center of the courtyard, both his brawny arms braced against it.

Eliab nodded a greeting as David entered. "I hoped you'd come early."

David pulled his cloak tighter around his shoulders. Was it the cold, or the fact that a murderer lingered in their ranks that made him shiver?

The three of them stood in silence as they waited for mourners to trickle in. Absalom was the first of his sons to arrive. His dark tresses hung in a tangled mess around his tearstained face. He ran to David, as he did when he was a child, threw his arms around his neck, and sobbed.

His elder brother, Amnon, appeared shortly after. He scoffed at his brother's emotional display, but his clothes were torn and dirty and his typical grin absent from his bearded face. Even Tamar's appearance didn't bring it back, as it always did.

"May Adonai bring you comfort, my lord." Abigail

bowed as she entered the courtyard. The wisdom shining from her brown eyes was still the most lovely thing about her. Her stance reminded him of the first time he laid eyes on her. She was much younger then, but she had knelt before him in the same manner, begging him to be merciful to her household despite her husband's foolish actions. He'd admired her then, as he did now.

Their son, Daniel, trailed her. He said nothing, only nodded with lips clamped tight. His eyes were soft and innocent, like Abigail's. No malice, no murder lurked in them.

For a moment, David's resolve faltered. Surely, none of his children were at fault. How could his sons kill their own flesh and blood? But what if they had? He couldn't risk a bloodthirsty individual gaining the throne. What would he do if he failed to find the culprit? The responsibility of exposing her killer weighed heavier than even the grief in his heart.

Eliab tugged on David's sleeve. "It is time to begin."

Abiathar, the priest, stood before the family and unrolled a scroll. "Blessed art thou, O Lord, King of the Universe, that giveth life and taketh it again."

Grit lanced David's knees as he dropped to the ground. He dug his fingers into the dirt and poured it over his head. Tears warmed his cheeks, and a knot tightened his stomach. Yes, God gave life or took it...but why did He have to take her *now*?

His head fell back, and he stared at the clouds dotting the sky. "The fairest and most pleasant among the daughters of Judah has been slain. Let not the sun shine over Bethlehem. Let not the rain quench the earth. Let the earth mourn for her, as does the House of David. Cry aloud sons of Jerusalem! For so loyal was the wife of Jesse in her love toward her children! And her service toward the House of Israel. Her hoary head be blessed forever and ever."

"Amen."

David hardly heard the echo of the mourners as he fell upon the ground and wept, his tears making puddles in the dust. When at last his tears ran dry, he summoned his strength and stood. He stumbled toward Imah's casket and grasped one end.

Adonijah, with his sackcloth and bare feet, stepped forward and gripped the other end. David's brothers lined up at the sides, and together they lifted the box and exited the courtyard.

David's other sons, concubines, and the rest of the mourners trailed them, weeping and casting dust into the air. The stench of ashes and sackcloth followed them all the way to the tomb. Their footsteps echoed off the cave walls as they entered. When they laid the casket upon its resting place, an eerie thud reverberated through the cavern.

Running his hands over the smooth wood, David leaned down and planted a kiss upon the lid. "I love you, Imah. May Abraham hold you tightly to his bosom."

He stood at the door of the tomb as his sons filed by, paying their last respects to their savta. Some had tears, others only grim lines on their faces, but all seemed sincere.

When the last one had gone, David embraced Eliab. "I don't know, brother. I've found nothing to raise my suspicions. The closer I watch them, the more convinced I am that they didn't do it."

"There is no way we can tell. I haven't slept since her passing trying to think of a way to find her killer, but there just isn't one." Eliab squeezed his shoulder. "Be careful, my brother. We don't know what, or who, may be next."

*****

Several weeks passed, as did the period of mourning. The Almighty heard David's prayers and spared Nun's life. Each day when David checked on him, he showed signs of improvement. By the time they resumed work on the swaddling clothes, the weaver had recovered enough to work a few hours each day.

The garment was coming together beautifully. David oft found Bathsheba sitting and watching the threads weave together and the exquisite fabric materialize. Six colors faded one into the other with the seventh color, yellow, forming a six-point star with a long tail in the center. Bathsheba traced the outline with her finger.

David leaned down and kissed the top of her head. "It won't be long now. Our son will be coming into the world soon."

She rested her hands on her bulging belly and smiled. "Yes, my lord. I am anxious for the day. But we must wait until his royal garment is ready for him."

"How much more time do you anticipate, Nun?"

The weaver bit his lip. "If I don't run into any more problems, I would say two weeks."

"Good. But two weeks will still be too soon for our little one, my dear." David grasped her hand and held it to his lips. "Try to hold on a little longer. You have a couple months yet to go."

With a gentle tug on her hand, he led his wife outside. Their steps echoed on the tile floor as they walked down the corridor. "You are happy then, with Nun's work so far, my wife?"

"Oh, yes. The fabric is beautiful. Unlike anything I've seen."

A satisfied smile stretched his lips. This was exactly what he'd been aiming for. How he loved to see her happy. "So, what should we name this special child the Almighty has blessed us with? What do you think of Solomon? It means peace."

Bathsheba stopped. A pained expression contorted her face. Her hands clutched her belly.

"What's wrong?" He sprang closer, supporting her with both hands on her upper arms.

"I...I don't..."

Her breathing rasped, grew heavy, and she gritted her teeth. Pain twisted her face yet deeper, and she doubled over.

"David, help me!"

In one swift movement, he swept her into his arms. With firm steps, he carried her toward her chamber, trying to think despite his stuttering heart.

"Yahweh, please have mercy. Ahithophel, Ahithophel, come quickly." David nearly stumbled. A thick liquid trickled down his arm. *Yahweh!* "Someone get the midwife. Bring her now!"

Bathsheba moaned as he set her on the bed. A large reddish splotch formed beneath her. His chest constricted as images of her last labor leached into his mind. He gripped her hand and held his breath, waiting for her pain-filled eyes to meet his.

He squeezed her hand tighter. "Hold on, Bathsheba. Hold on, my love."

Another wave of pain gripped her. He remained at her side as servants ran back and forth bringing water, clean cloths, and other supplies.

An eternity passed before the midwife arrived. David sprang to his feet as she entered. "We were walking in the hall when pain seized her. She's bleeding heavily."

Glancing at the tormented woman on the bed, the midwife gave David a gentle push. "It'd be best if you wait outside, my lord."

David's fists dug into his hair as his feet carried him outside the room. He choked, trying to breathe. This was too much like last time.

God of Abraham, Isaac, and Jacob have mercy. Do not take this child from me. Have I not already paid the price for my iniquity? Remember it not, O Lord, and save Your anointed. Hear, and come quickly, Lord of Hosts.

The first child had been cursed. David fasted for days, praying the Lord would somehow allow the child to live. Yet he died. Just as Nathan said.

Nathan.

Frantic, David spun around. A guard slumped against a wall, fiddling with the leather handle of his spear. "You!" The guard snapped to attention at his growl. "Go quick as you can and bring Nathan the Prophet to me. Do not return without him."

The soldier nodded and headed for the courtyard.

"Run, you fool! A single moment can mean life or death."

*****

Second thoughts invaded Absalom's mind. This was a risky move. If Nathan told the king he had come to him asking a curse upon the child, who knew what the king may do.

He paced as he waited for the prophet. He should sit, but where? The humble dwelling offered little in the way of comforts—a threadbare rug on the dirt floor, a small clay oven, and one room off to the side. He shivered. A chill from the night before still radiated off the stone walls. In the absence of chairs, with caution, Absalom balanced on the lone meal barrel.

Finally, the prophet entered. Dried grass clung to the seat of his robe. Some fluttered off as he bent to brace his staff against the door before facing Absalom. "Greetings, son of David."

"I have been waiting for you."

The seer looked straight into his eyes. "Not even a prince comes before prayers to the Lord."

"All right then, do you know why I'm here?"

A slight smile rested on Nathan's lips. "I think so, but do enlighten me."

"My father's newest wife, Bathsheba, is with child. Again."

Nathan arched a brow. "Does this surprise you?"

"Well—no. What does surprise me is that God would allow a child to bless their marriage after all that has taken place. Does the Almighty condone the king's actions in taking Bathsheba? Will not Yahweh curse this child as well?"

The seer's eyes narrowed as he leaned forward. "Is this about justice for sin, or about your ascent to the throne?"

Exposed. He should have known a seer would see through him. Absalom let out a breath. "I have reason to believe my father will try to make this child his heir, but that right should go to him last of all. This child will be the seventh-born son. He should be last in line to the throne. I am third born, with my mother also of royal blood as the princess of Geshur. This child's mother is a commoner, the wife of a poor Hittite. Does not the Lord desire someone of royal blood and a capable mind to rule His chosen people?"

"The Lord desires someone devoted to Him to rule His people."

"Am I not devoted to Him? I have kept the law. I have made the sacrifices. I worship every week."

"It is not eye-service that pleases the Lord, but singleness of heart. Yes, Absalom, I have heard from the Lord, and He has commanded me to visit your father and speak regarding the child."

"Thank you."

A shout came from outside. "Man of God."

Absalom followed Nathan outside. A palace guard ran to the prophet and fell at his feet, panting. "King David asks you to come as fast as possible. He says it is a matter of life and death."

The guard glanced at Absalom. A flicker of suspicion lingering in his eye. His presence at Nathan's dwelling did seem a bit odd.

"If my father requests haste, then take my horse. I'll follow on foot." That should squelch anyone's suspicion.

"That would be best." The guard nodded.

"If you insist, I would be glad to ride." Nathan mounted the stallion. "I'll see you at the palace."

Dust wafted as Nathan galloped away. Absalom turned to the guard still standing next to him. "It looks like you and I have a long walk ahead of us."

"The walk is not too far. I was able to run all the way here, but it was good of you to let the man of God take your horse. Your father seemed in great distress."

"I admire your loyalty and obedience in coming so speedily. I will make mention of it to the king. Tell me, what is wrong with my father?"

"I can't say for certain, but he said a moment could make the difference in life and death."

Life and death...you don't say. "How did you happen upon my father in such distress?"

Had he known what a flood of words that question released, Absalom wouldn't have asked. The rest of the journey, the guard went on about his station at the palace, his family situation, and his loyalty to the crown. By the time they reached the palace, even Absalom's flattering ears had about enough. He exhaled when the guard bid him a quick farewell and returned to his post.

It wasn't hard to find Nathan and David. Servants milled about like ants upon their collapsed colony.

As he peered into the chamber, his father's pleading voice rose above all. "The child has come too soon. Please, Nathan, inquire of the Lord for the child; that he may live."

The prophet's low voice echoed in the small room. "Thus saith the Lord God of Israel: I have seen the son of David my servant, this child he has called Solomon, and I love him. Therefore he shall be called Jedidiah, for he is beloved of the Lord."[9]

"Then, my son will live?"

"Your son will live."

David clasped his hands together. "Blessed be the name of the Lord our God who has heard the cry of His servants. The son of David lives."

Absalom slipped out of the room. How could this have happened? He had spoken to the man of God and been assured he would honor his request. Instead, the seer blessed the child and named him The Beloved. How would he ever gain his throne with Bathsheba's son—and the blessing of the prophet—in his way?

*****

Tears of joy and relief streamed down David's cheeks as he accepted the swaddling clothes from Nun. He had barely finished them in time for the circumcision ceremony. Lifting his infant son from his cradle, David

[9] 2 Sam 12:25

wrapped the child in royal cloth so exquisite none could doubt its significance. With pride swelling his chest, he handed the babe to Bathsheba, and they walked together to the cedar hall.

The prophet Nathan stood at the door. "I've come to witness the circumcision of the king's son." A meaningful gleam rested in the seer's eye. The prophet knew. Solomon would be his heir.

"Thank you, Prophet." David clasped his shoulder. "It means much to me."

Nathan held the door for Bathsheba and David. The hall glowed with the warm light of lamps and smelled of olive oil. Ahithophel and his wife stood dutifully to one side.

The priest smiled as they entered. "Mozel tov, my lord."

"Thank you, Abiathar." David couldn't hold back a grin. "How many circumcisions have you performed for me, my friend?"

"More than I care to keep track of. Shall we begin?"

"Yes, the witnesses are here." He motioned to Nathan, Ahithophel, and his wife.

"Very well then." Abiathar unfolded the cloth containing his instruments for the circumcision. "Bring the babe."

Ahithophel's wife took the child from Bathsheba and placed him in her husband's arms, who carried him to the table erected for the ceremony. David stood beside the priest and smiled down at his newborn son. Solomon's lips puckered as the priest unwrapped his warm cocoon.

"Blessed are You, Lord our God, King of the universe, Who has sanctified us with His commandments and commanded us concerning circumcision." Abiathar held out his hand, and David lifted the knife from the table and placed it in his waiting palm.

The babe's whimpers escalated to squeals as the priest began the circumcision. David raised his voice above his son's cries to voice his portion of the blessing. "Blessed are You, Lord our God, King of the universe, Who has sanctified us with His commandments and commanded us to enter him into the Covenant of Abraham our father."

"Just as he has entered into the Covenant, so may he enter into Torah, into marriage, and into good deeds." The witnesses recited in unison.

"What will you call the child?" Abiathar asked as he wiped his hands.

"He shall be called Solomon Jedidiah." David's gaze caught Bathsheba's. One green eye winked.

The priest picked up Solomon and bounced. "All right, little one, it's all over now."

The babe screamed louder.

Abiathar chuckled. "Return the infant to his mother. My comfort is not sufficient."

From the priest, to Ahithophel, his wife...but when Solomon reached Bathsheba's arms, he quieted.

The hall doors opened, and Ahithophel shouted, "Blessed be Solomon Jedidiah, son of David, king of Israel!"

The waiting crowd cheered. "Long live Prince Solomon. Long live King David."

Then the festivities began. True to his word, David sent a proclamation to the troops encamped against Rabbah-Ammon commanding they cease from fighting in honor of Solomon's birth, and the people of Jerusalem feasted for a month on the most scrumptious foods the treasury could afford.[10]

*****

Circa 969 B.C.

Sitting in a small room inside his house, Absalom ordered all the windows shut and all visitors turned away. Across the table from him sat his mother and Ahithophel. [11]

---

[10] 2 Sam 12:24-25

"Absalom, I have served your father for many years as his faithful and trusted aide. I served him during his most glorious years. But he has grown arrogant and foolish. It is time for the throne to be passed on. With Amnon dead, and Daniel's ineligibility, you stand as next in line."

Bowing his head in a gesture of humility, Absalom replied, "I am honored by your loyalty, Ahithophel, and I appreciate your insight. I too share your sentiments. So, what do you suggest?"

"Though the favor for you is great, it will not be easy for you to take the throne. Your father is no longer young. Any day he may go the way of his fathers. Then the Swaddling Clothes decree will be read. If that happens…" Ahithophel shrugged. No need to say more.

"But the hearts of the people are for me. Why would they accept Solomon, even with the swaddling clothes, when I am the heir apparent?"

Ahithophel sighed and rubbed his balding head. "I have seen the decree. It details every symbolism used in the creation of the swaddling clothes. When your father made it, he wasn't making a cloth, but a prophecy and a blessing. Nathan the Prophet is also for Solomon and will convince the people he is God's chosen heir."

Absalom rose and paced across the plank floor. "So

[11] 2 Sam 15:12

what should we do?"

"My son, after more than forty years of preparation, the time is finally right for you to claim your throne." Maacah's dark eyes glimmered beneath her wrinkling brows. "We've been waiting for this time all your life."

"You have to become king before they can issue the Swaddling Clothes decree. We must act at once."

"All right, Ahithophel. Let's formulate a plan."[12]

---

[12] 2 Sam 15 Absalom conspires against David. Absalom is slain during the conflict.

Chapter Five

Circa 962 B.C.

Leaning heavily on her cane, Maacah hobbled across the harem courtyard. King David's health was failing. She would soon follow him in death, but first, she had an old score to settle. She and Absalom had been so close to their goal. He had slain his older brother, Amnon, and became heir apparent. Yet the swaddling clothes again threatened him. They had to act before the king announced the swaddling clothes pertained to his heir. How the people had favored Absalom. In her mind's eye, she saw the happy faces of the women as Absalom was crowned in Hebron. Her heart still thrilled at the memory of her son with the crown upon his head. Yet now, he was dead, and her hopes with him.

What would a new king do to her? The mother of a conspirator? But more than fear for her life drove her to this errand. She would avenge her son upon David and Solomon. Perhaps her son could no longer reign, but the son of that woman, Bathsheba, would never reign either. Of that, she would make sure.

She stopped in front of the door to the chambers belonging to Haggith, another of David's wives, the mother of his fourth born son, and knocked. A servant opened the door and, raising an eyebrow, stepped aside for her to enter.

"I wish to see the lady Haggith. I have an urgent matter to discuss with her."

The maid disappeared for a moment, and then returned, summoning her into a room. Haggith sat cross-legged at a low table. Her turquoise robe matched the color of her eyes, bordered by thick lashes and raven-black hair with a lining of silver. The wrinkles by her eyes deepened when she looked up at Maacah. "What a rare occasion this is, Lady Maacah. To what do I owe this honor?"

The hint of sarcasm in her voice didn't shake Maacah's resolve. "I am here to help you, my lady, but if you insist on being rude, I will leave."

Haggith gestured to the seat across from her.

"The matter I wish to discuss is a private one, my lady." Maacah glanced at the maid who stood at attention in the corner.

"You may go, Rebekah. I will call you if you're needed."

The maid dismissed herself with a slight bow, and Maacah sat on the plush rug facing Haggith. "How is your son?"

"Adonaijah is well."

Maacah nodded. "That is good to hear. I suppose you have heard of our lord, King David's situation? He has been very ill. His body will no longer hold heat. He lays beneath piles of blankets, yet shivers from cold."[13]

Still eyeing her guest suspiciously, Haggith bobbed her head. "So I have heard. My son is prepared to lead the kingdom when our lord rests with his fathers."[14]

Maacah's lips twitched toward a smile. At last, they had come to the subject. "That is what I wished to discuss with you, my lady. I have information you do not yet know."

Haggith's brow knit together. "Such as?"

---

[13] 1 Kings 1:1-4

[14] 1 Kings 1:5

"David will not name your son heir to the throne."

The woman's turquoise eyes searched her face. "Please explain."

"The king intends to pass the throne to Solomon, the son of Bathsheba. This conspiracy has been working in the palace since before the child was born. Absalom and I did everything we could to stop it, but we couldn't succeed."

Questions and concern etched into Haggith's countenance, deepening the lines on her forehead.

"You do not believe me." Maacah helped herself to the bowl of fruit on the table. She bit into an apple, the crisp crunch adding to the tension in the room. "Was it not suspicious when the king brought weavers from all over the kingdom, and merchants from all over the world, to fashion swaddling clothes for the newborn prince? Has he done that for any of his other sons?" Maacah paused for effect. "He created the swaddling clothes as a blessing and a symbol of Solomon's ascent to the throne. Any day now, the king will announce his chosen heir and the significance and blessing of the swaddling clothes and their design. If you want your son to reign, you must act before they have a chance."

Haggith sat back and crossed her arms. She watched Maacah for a long moment. Taking another bite, Maacah waited. She swallowed, and at last, her host spoke. "How do I know what you're saying is true?"

Maacah tried to suppress a grin. "You could wait until it happens and your son is trumped by his younger and less eligible brother."

"My son is a good man. The king has never rebuked him."[15] Haggith bit her lip. "He is close friends with Joab, captain of the host, and Abiathar, the priest. I will have him counsel with them on this matter." Leaning forward, Haggith eyes locked on hers. "Why have you come to tell me this?"

"When my son, Absalom, was still alive, I swore to him that the son of this common woman, Bathsheba, would never reign over him. I seek to keep my word to the son I still mourn. I also ask that when your son comes to the throne, he would remember my service and allow me and my daughter to live peaceably."

Haggith nodded. "I will speak to him on your behalf."

Rising with the aid of her cane, Maacah nodded a goodbye to her host. Then slipped out the door.

*****

"Adonaijah reigns? But, Nathan, how can this be?" Fear rose like a cold mist in Bathsheba's heart. Soon her husband would go to be with his fathers, and she and Solomon would be seen as outlaws in the land. She turned

[15] 1 Kings 1:6-7

to her son sitting by her side. Yes, Solomon was still young, but old enough to claim the throne.[16]

"My lady, even as we speak, Adonaijah is near the Serpent Stone with Joab, captain of the host, and Abiathar, the priest, offering sacrifices. He has invited his younger brothers and all the men of Judah to celebrate with him."

She ran a wrinkled hand through her hair, fingers catching in still-red strands. "But David promised me Solomon would be his heir. How could he have named Adonaijah as king?"

"Adonaijah is self-proclaimed, my lady. Our king knows nothing of this."

"What can we do?"

"Bathsheba, you still hold the king's favor, his love for you has not faded with his health. Go to him and tell him what has happened. Ask him to fulfill his promise to you, and declare Solomon as king. I will follow to bear witness to what you have said."

"Nathan," Solomon spoke up. "Do you believe Yahweh would have me to reign? I am younger than my brother and not as qualified to rule."

The man of God placed a hand on her son's shoulder. "Solomon, the Lord has loved you since before you were even born. You will be king of Israel, and all that your

[16] 1 Kings 1:11-14

father has prophesied of you will come to pass. Adonai has chosen you to build His temple. Have faith and serve the Lord your God faithfully."

Bathsheba inhaled a deep breath. "Very well. Let us go to the king."

*****

Raising her hand in an effort to steady her flittering heart, Bathsheba stood outside King David's chamber. So many times she had entered this room and seen his face light with a smile warmer than a summer day. Now, she would enter to see an old man, his many years evidenced in his face and eyes.

She raised her hand and tapped on the cedar door.

The young maiden, who tended the king, opened, and David's frail voice came from within. "Who is there, Abishag?"

Bathsheba entered the room. David's squinting eyes relaxed, and his lips softened into a smile as he sank back on the cushions.

"Ah, Bathsheba, my beloved. I would know you anywhere. Come closer, my darling. My eyes are fading."

Her heart squeezed, and a tear slid down her cheek. Oh, how she still loved him, and how painful it was to see him this way. A conspirator reigned over his country, yet he was so weak and ill, he didn't even know it. She stepped into a ray of light streaming in the window a few feet from where her lord lay.

"You have aged gracefully. You're still as lovely as I remember." David held out his feeble hand to her.

Falling on her knees, she clasped his hand in both of hers and left upon it a lingering kiss before holding it to her cheek.

David's brow dropped when he touched the tears streaming down her wrinkled face. "What is it, my love? Why have you come?"

"My lord, you swore by the Lord your God unto me, your handmaid, that our son, Solomon, would surely reign after you and he would sit on your throne. But now, Adonaijah reigns, and my lord, you don't know it." David's head cocked, but he said nothing, so she continued, "He has made many sacrifices of sheep and oxen. He has called together the sons of the king, and Abiathar, the priest, and Joab, captain of the host. But Solomon, your servant, he has not invited. Now, my king, the eyes of all Israel rest upon you to see who you will name as successor to your throne." [17]

"Adonaijah proclaims himself king, without my

[17] 1 Kings 1:15-21

consent?"

"My lord, I am afraid you shall soon leave me to sleep with your fathers, leaving Solomon and me as offenders in the new king's eyes."

Another knock rattled the door.

The maid opened it. "It is Nathan the Prophet, my lord."

"Allow me to speak with the man of God, Bathsheba. Then I will settle this matter with a decree that cannot be revoked."

With a nod, Bathsheba rose and left the room to wait in the hall. She leaned her head against the wall, the scent of cedar surrounding her, and whispered a prayer. "God of Abraham, show favor this day to Solomon Thy beloved and be kind unto king David Thine anointed. Deliver us out of the hand of Adonaijah."

*****

A dagger of pain lanced David's heart as memories flooded his mind. He could see Amnon, Absalom, and Adonaijah practicing with their swords in the courtyard. Himself teaching them how to fight like a king, how to thrust, and when to have mercy. Images of their smiling faces haunted him. Amnon and Absalom were now dead, and he still mourned them. He still felt the stinging anger upon hearing Absalom had been slain to halt the conspiracy, despite his request to spare him. Would Adonaijah suffer the same fate?

David struggled to lift himself so he could sit up on his bed as the prophet entered. His teeth chattered, and he clamped his muscles tight to keep his body from shivering as he rose out of the blankets.

[18]Nathan bowed with his face toward the ground. "My lord king, have you declared that Adonaijah would reign after you and should inherit your throne? For today, he has summoned the people and holds a celebration, and they all shout 'God save King Adonaijah.' Please tell me, my lord, is this thing of your doing and you did not tell me?"

"Nathan, my friend, I had hoped you would tell me this thing was not true. It grieves my heart, and I am too old to bear the burdens of a king." David waved a hand at his servant. "Abishag, bring Bathsheba back in."

Mustering what strength he had left, David stood on shaky feet as his wife approached. The fear and concern in her eyes gave him courage as he spoke. "My beloved, as the Lord lives and has redeemed my soul out of all

[18] 1 Kings 1:22-31

distress, even as I swore to you by the LORD God of Israel, saying, assuredly Solomon your son shall reign after me, and he shall sit upon my throne in my stead; even so will I do this day."

Bathsheba fell at his feet. Relief smoothed the beautiful planes of her face. "Thank you. May my lord, King David, live forever."

David summoned Zadok, the priest, along with Benaiah, the captain of the host, so he could command them concerning his heir. He would make Solomon king in his place if it was his final act as king. [19]

When they assembled before him, David limped to his olive wood chest and opened it. He pulled from its hold a long strip of well-crafted, multicolored cloth and held it up before them.

"This cloth was crafted especially for the son who would be my heir. These swaddling clothes have, woven into every thread, a special blessing and symbol for the man who will inherit my throne." David offered the cloth to Zadok.

The priest smoothed the cloth with his palm. "The seven colors of the rainbow, a sign of peace, and of a father's blessing on his son."

"These are Solomon's, aren't they?" Nathan fingered

[19] 1 Kings 1:32-36

the scarlet threads.

"Yes." David bent and lifted a scroll from the chest. "This decree I intended to have issued upon my death, but it seems the time has come to make it known to the people. Take this cloth and tie it upon a rod. Lead Solomon to Gihon upon my own mule shouting 'behold the banner of the king of Israel'. Then Zadok, as priest, and Nathan, as the prophet of God, anoint Solomon there as king over Israel and let the people say 'God save King Solomon.' Let the words of this decree be read in the ears of the people. Then bring him and sit him upon my throne that he may rule and judge over the house of Judah and over all of Israel."

Benaiah lifted the scroll from David's hands. "Amen. May Adonai the God of my lord the king, confirm it."

Part Two

Chapter Six

Circa 607 B.C.

"So Solomon was proclaimed king of Israel and reigned over all the land for forty years. During his reign, Israel prospered, for Solomon was given the gift of wisdom. Everything David, his father, prophesied of him came to pass. And he built the magnificent temple. Ever since then, this star has been our banner, and so we keep this cloth locked away and protected, Salathiel. Because this cloth is a sign that we are of the chosen royal lineage."

Jehoiachin's young son fingered the fabric that still held the same brilliance it had so many years ago. "Were you wrapped in this cloth, Abba?"

"Yes, my son, as were you." Jehoiachin thumbed his son's nose.

"Is that why the Babylonians bla-siege the city?"

The king tried to smile as he folded the fabric and placed it in its wooden box. "No, son. The Babylonians don't care about the swaddling clothes. Nebuchadnezzar only cares about money and power. He besieges the city because he wants our money, and he wants us to be his slaves."

"Abba, I'm hungry."

Jehoiachin's mouth formed a thin line. "I know. So am I."

So were all the people in Jerusalem. Nebuchadnezzar's siege had cut off their food supplies, and their stores were running out. One option remained. He would have to give himself up, surrender Jerusalem, or the city would perish. How could he have been foolish enough to break his word to the king of Babylon? But his confidence in Egypt had proven in vain, just as the prophet of God had predicted. If only he had listened to the prophet…but it was too late now.[20]

The king began to close the box cradling the swaddling clothes, but he stopped and opened it again.

[20] 2 Kings 24:6-15

"Salathiel, come here."

His son obediently stepped close to him. Taking the cloth from its box, Jehoiachin folded it into a sash and wrapped it around his son's waist underneath his outer robe. "Whatever happens in the next few hours, and the next few years, you keep this cloth close to you. Someday, you may need to prove you are of the lineage of David, and you can show the swaddling clothes as evidence. Maybe someday the Lord will forgive me for my evil ways and have mercy upon His people and restore us to our kingdom."

Salathiel nodded. "What are you going to do, Abba?"

He swallowed hard. "The only thing I can do. I'm going to surrender."

Footsteps thudded at the doorway, and the general strode into the room. "Everything is as you have commanded, my lord. Are you ready to do this?"

"No. But it must be done." Jehoiachin rose and, giving his son one last pat on the head, followed his general out of the room.

*****

Watching his father from the window, Salathiel touched the silken fabric that lined his waist. Such an important token, and Abba had given it to him. What did Abba think would happen? What would the king of Babylon do when Abba surrendered?

Below, his father mounted his horse. Several men went in front of him, one of them holding a white flag, and another holding the flag of Israel with a star similar to the one on Solomon's swaddling clothes. The flags faded into the distance as they rode toward the city gate.

A loud grumble came from his stomach. He had never been this hungry before. Turning from the window, he set off to find his mother. Perhaps she would be able to offer him some food, or at least a sip of wine to settle his stomach.

A strange quietness filled the harem as he wandered through it in search of Imah. He found her, bustling about in her chamber. "What are you doing, Imah?"

She jumped and pressed one hand to her heart. "Oh, Salathiel, don't sneak up on me. Do you want to kill your imah with fright?"

"I'm sorry. Imah, I'm hungry. Isn't there anything to eat at all?"

His mother plopped onto a stool. "Not unless you can eat my jewels. Oh, here I am trying to hide a few things away so the Babylonians won't take them from me, but what does it matter when my children are starving and the kingdom is rent from our hands?"

"Don't cry, Imah. Abba says we might have to leave, but we'll come back someday. And they will all know we are supposed to be the king and queen because I have this." Holding open his robe, his chest puffed out, he displayed the sash.

"You sweet boy." Imah gathered him in her arms and held him close.

A stampede of horse hooves clobbered in the courtyard. Shouts in a language Salathiel didn't understand accompanied them. Someone banged on their door.

Imah squeezed him tighter. "Be brave, my son. Remember you are a prince of the house of David." She then rose to answer the shouts. The enormous wooden door burst open before she could lift the latch, and it knocked her to the ground.

"Imah!"

Babylonian soldiers with strange helmets entered and gestured at his mother, then him. Grabbing his arm, one dragged him outside. Salathiel's brothers and sisters and the servant children all huddled in a group at the center of the courtyard. Enemy soldiers, too numerous for him to count, swarmed in and out of every door threshing out people and valuables as they went.

A soldier shoved him toward the group of trembling children and uttered in heavily accented Hebrew, "Stay."

Stumbling to his feet, Salathiel spun around as panic filled his being. "Imah? Imah, where are you?"

"I'm here, my son. Be brave. You are a prince." Her voice was faint, and he could not tell from which direction it had come. But he heaved a deep breath, summoned all the courage his seven-year-old heart could muster, and held his head high.

As the Babylonians piled his father's belongings onto carts, whooping and laughing at each treasure.

Soon a Babylonian soldier came with a long rope. The man tied a knot around Salathiel's wrists. The soldier tied one of his sisters next to him, leaving about an arm's length of rope between them. The man went down the line until he ran out of rope.

The cord tightened around Salathiel's wrists. He wriggled them, trying to loosen its hold, but to no avail.

After what seemed an eternity, the soldiers came back around and began yelling at them in their strange tongue. A soldier grabbed Salathiel's arm and yanked him to his feet. The rest of the children followed his lead, scrambling to stand before the temperamental outsiders could clout them. The soldier shoved him and pointed toward the gate, again muttering something in his foreign language.

Salathiel began walking, keeping his head held high. They walked until he was sure the bottoms of his sandals were worn through. Finally night fell, and they halted. A Babylonian captain stepped in front of him. The man's harsh eyes narrowed, and the steel hanging from his helmet clanked like the chimes hanging from the palace balcony. He whipped out his sword.

A gasp escaped Salathiel's lungs. His hands instinctively shielded his face, awaiting the deathblow.

A grunt, and the sword whooshed through the air...landing in the sand with a dull thud. The steel grated against the sand as the Babylonian drew a large circle on the ground. He clutched Salathiel's tunic and pushed him inside the circle. "Sit."

Allowing his weary body to crumple, Salathiel obeyed.

The captain laughed. "Hebrew is like dog." He turned to the other children, who watched with wide eyes. He tilted his head toward Salathiel, and the children obeyed his silent command, huddling inside the circle.

Salathiel waited, hoping they would free them from the rope pinching his wrists, but they didn't. Instead, the soldiers tossed bread at them, laughing as his brothers and sisters scrambled and fell trying to catch it with their hands tied together. Though it wasn't much, the bread was more food than they had during the weeks of the siege.

When the bread had been devoured, one soldier brought a bucket with a ladle and allowed the children a drink. Then the soldiers took turns keeping watch over them throughout the night, leaving no opportunity for escape.

A blow to the stomach awakened Salathiel. His eyes snapped open to the scruffy face of the Babylonian soldier. "Wake, Hebrew. Time move."

The sun was just beginning to lighten the camp. He glanced around, trying to regain his composure and spotted a familiar form.

Imah.

She stood like a wilted flower. Dark circles surrounded her reddened eyes. Dried blood caked the side of her head. He called out to her, but her weary gaze remained latched the ground.

Anger rose within his small chest. He was the heir of the kingdom of Israel. She — as his mother — should be cared for, watched after until she died of a ripe old age. How quickly their destined future changed.

Someday, he would rise against his captors, slay them all, carrying only their wives and children away captive. He would return to Jerusalem in triumph to reign over

Israel in their homeland. Yes. Someday, he would find a way.

Many nights passed in the manner as the first, except he didn't see his mother again. Each morning he looked for her among the throng. He tried to keep count of how many mornings passed, but the longer they walked in the hot sun, the foggier the memory became. Though his feet ached and he felt he could go no farther, he refused to show weariness. He was a prince of Judah, and he would not display weakness before his enemies. Instead, he observed them.

By listening to their conversation, he learned a few of their words. They must be getting close to their destination, because the soldiers began to smile. They became less agitated with their captives, and their Babylonian chatter became quick and more expressive.

At a chant from the soldiers, Salathiel raised his head. A large, sand-colored structure loomed on the horizon. As they neared, he distinguished an enormous bridge leading to what must be the Babylonian capital. Palm trees and towers lined the walls, and tiny ships floated on the river beneath the bridge. The gate opened as the troop approached it, and the sounding of trumpets and shouts of thousands rang through the sky. Salathiel's heart thundered, and he froze, absorbing the frightening images of Babylonian gods etched into the walls, pillars, and buildings.

"Move, Hebrew." One of the soldiers gave him a shove, and they marched forward again.

As they entered the city, Babylonians lined the streets. They cheered even louder while soldiers paraded their prisoners past. The crowd sneered and threw produce and garbage at the captives as they paraded through the streets. At last, they reached the temple of Bel, a god familiar to Salathiel. Many of the harem women possessed his images, and his father had built a grove to Bel outside Jerusalem for them.

The soldiers led their captives to the top of the temple stairs and halted outside the golden doors. Salathiel turned. From the height of the temple, he could see the rest of the parade below. Heat rose to his face. His father's throne, golden ornaments, jeweled goblets, silver serving bowls, bronze lavers, even the Arc of the Covenant lumbered through the street, a display for even the most common heathen to smudge with his filthy fingertips.

Everything the Israelites ever loved, everything they treasured, had been carried away on the backs of Gentiles to far away Babylon. How could they ever regain everything they'd lost? He wiped his eyes with his fists. He wouldn't let the enemy to see him cry. It wasn't princely. But at that moment, he realized what it meant when his father said he was going to "surrender." He gave up everything.

What had befallen his parents? The last time he'd seen his mother was when they stopped for water many days ago. He hadn't seen his father since he rode away under the flag of Israel.

When the final cart of treasures reached the bottom of the temple steps, the trumpeting ceased. The great golden doors yawned open like a beast ready to devour them.

The captain nudged Salathiel's shoulder. "Inside."

He inched forward. His heart constricted. The hall was narrow…and dark.

"Move, Hebrew."

A torch ignited, and he followed a soldier into a cavernous chamber overlaid with gold. The torchlight reflected off the walls, ceiling, and floor. He squinted, trying to identify two imposing figures at the far side.

With his boots clicking on the gold floor, the captain approached the figures and bowed low. Salathiel didn't understand all he said, but he heard the word that he supposed meant "captives" and identified Jerusalem.

Jewelry tinkled as the figure came forward. Whether male or female, he couldn't tell. Gold and precious jewels draped it from head to foot, and its clothing reminded him of the serpents living in the stone walls of their palace. Was this their priest?

"Very good." The voice purred slow and nasally, but in Hebrew. The eyes were black, surrounded by yellow where most had white. Perhaps it wasn't human at all, but a monster. "That one." It pointed to one of the young girls. "Take her for the sacrifice."

Salathiel's heart lurched. His father had so many wives and concubines, he didn't know all his siblings, but this girl was his kindred. She shrieked as a soldier grasped her arm and dragged her toward the door.

"No!" He struggled against the ropes, but they pinched tighter.

"Silence, Hebrew." The captain's nails dug into his shoulder. "You want be next?"

Helplessness bled life from his heart as the doors closed, locking him in. And the girl out.

Suddenly, four hands groped at his tunic. Two soldiers stripped off his outer robe, exposing his colorful sash. One grabbed it and jabbered in Babylonian.

"No! No, you can't take this." He dropped to the ground and curled his arms around his middle. "You have taken everything else from me, but you cannot take my sash."

The soldiers laughed. One held Salathiel's arms, and

the other took the swaddling cloth.

"Give it back! Please, give it back."

Again, the Babylonian laughed and dangled the sash in front of him. Salathiel lunged for it, his fingers almost touching the scarlet edge, but the soldier jerked it away. With another evil laugh, he disappeared, and the cloth with him.

Salathiel crumpled to the ground, the cold like ice against his knees. He pressed his palms against the gold and stared at his reflection. He no longer cared about appearances. The Babylonians had taken everything from him, even the proof of his royalty. Why act like a prince when no one would ever know he had been one? Here he stood, stripped of even his clothing before his enemy.

A short, fat man with a gray beard stepped in front of the children. He spoke broken Hebrew with an accent that made every word despicable to Salathiel. "Welcome to the great Babylon. Whatever you were before you came here does not matter. Here, you are servants." He pointed to a pile of plain servant's garments. "Take one of those and put it on. You will be divided up to serve in the house of Bel and in the house of the king, Nebuchadnezzar."

Salathiel jumped on the man, fists flying into his pudgy nose. The next thing he knew, he was lying on the floor with the fat man staring at him. "Get used to looking up from the floor, you stupid Jew. You'll be doing that for the rest of your life."

Chapter Seven

Circa 536 B.C.

Lifting a heavy hand, Zerubbabel knocked on
Nehemiah's door. His friend soon answered.

"Shabbat shalom, Nehemiah."

"A peaceful Sabbath to you as well." His friend raised
an eyebrow. "You're early for the Torah reading. Is there
something wrong?"

Zerubbabel stepped inside and paced a few strides
before answering. "I had hoped to speak with you. My
heart is heavy within me. All my life I have served in the
palace, and now with my son coming of age, I see nothing
but the same future for him. How long will the Lord keep
us in captivity? How long must we bear the reproach of

our fathers?"

"I know this is difficult for you, my friend, but we cannot allow captivity to downcast our spirits. These heathens need to see that God's people can be joyous even in tribulation because our God lives. Adonai is with us, even in our captivity."

"For you to say so is easy, but I am of the royal line. My grandfather, Jehoiachin, surrendered the city and our temple. And for the sin of my grandfathers the Lord sold us into captivity. My people are desolate — enslaved — and I feel responsible."

"I too, long to see our people return to our homeland." Nehemiah's face sobered as he spoke. "To once again worship in Mount Zion. But we still have hope. The prophet left us a promise when he said 'If my people, who are called by my name, will repent and call upon me, then I will hear their cry and I will heal their land.' We have to hold to this promise."

"Then pray with me, my friend. My heart is so heavy it has sunk into my stomach and I cannot eat. Ever since my father was carried away as a small boy, he anticipated the day God would deliver us again to Jerusalem. He would take me on his knee every night when he finished serving at Nebuchadnezzar's table and tell me that one day we would again enter the holy city and rebuild the

Lord's temple."

His friend patted him on the shoulder. "I'm sure your father's passing has made it more vivid in your mind. I will both fast and pray with you."

Together they commenced the ceremonial cleansing. They dipped a cup into the basins and poured the water over their hands. Then as they dried their hands with a towel, they turned toward Jerusalem and recited a prayer. "Blessed art Thou, O Lord, King of the Universe who sanctifies us with His commandments and commands us concerning the washing of hands."

Gradually, other worshipers arrived and sat around the room to hear the words of the Torah. Ezra, their priest and scribe, stood and read from the book of the Lamentations of Jeremiah. Each word bore into Zerubbabel's soul.

When the priest finished his reading, Zerubbabel stood and strode to the center of the room.

"Brothers, my heart is heavy. For too long we have sojourned in Babylon, carried away as captives from our homeland. The Lord has pressed upon me a burden heavier than I can bare alone. So I ask you to share my burden and join me in fasting and pray the Lord will again turn His heart to His people and restore them to the Promised Land."

For a moment, the group was silent. Ezra rose. "I also share this heavy burden. I believe the time of our exodus is near. I will join you, Zerubbabel, in fasting and prayer."

Several men echoed Ezra's sentiments.

"Thank you, my brothers. I will ask you to fast starting at sundown. We will fast for three days, and then meet for prayer."

One man stood, his eyes wide. "You want us to fast for three days? My brother's son is having a wedding on the morrow. I cannot fast through it."

Zerubbabel returned his intent gaze. "Which is more important to you, Dathan? The salvation of Israel and our return to Jerusalem, or your stomach?" He scanned the room, meeting one set of eyes after another, seeing the turmoil of captivity, the longing for home, the sickness of the heart in many. A quickening of God touched his soul. "I will not force you to participate. But it is time for the Lord's people to be sober, to repent and seek after the Lord our God with all our hearts as our father David did. Nothing else will bring the mercy of God and the return to Jerusalem."

With a final prayer, the group concluded their Sabbath meeting. Zerubbabel walked home feeling comforted by the support of his brethren. But when he passed the temple of Bel, the pain of captivity tore through him, raw and angry. The huge ziggurat formed the center of all activity in Babylon. Legend told that it was based upon the Tower of Babel that the Babylonian king aspired to build when the people were all of one language. By God's grace, he never had to see the inside of it. But rumor claimed more than two hundred people served in there, trapped inside the dark pyramid their entire lives. How he hated living in a pagan land.

Please, Lord, God of Abraham, do not forsake Your people. Lead us again to Jerusalem that we may worship in Your temple.

He trudged through the streets to the stone hut he called his home. The interior was humble at best, with a cloth curtain to separate the only private chamber from the rest of the house. His two daughters played with dolls. His wife tended a fire in the tiny hearth, perspiration beading on her forehead while she knelt on the cobblestone floor.

"Abiud asked to visit Judah this afternoon. I allowed him to go."

Zerubbabel's chest tightened. "Geula, we have talked about this. We must keep Abiud out of sight as much as possible. Our son is now old enough to be called to serve the Babylonians. The longer we delay his assignment, the better. There's no telling what these pagans would have a twelve-year-old boy do."

His wife straightened, placing her hands on the small

of her back. "I'm sorry, Zerubbabel. He grew restless and grumpy. I had to do something, and I thought the Sabbath would be the best day for him to be out. No one could know he wasn't already employed by the king."

He sat on a stool and held his head in his hand. "He is a prince of the house of David, and yet he is destined to serve in whatever capacity his enemies determine. As am I. It isn't right. What else could they take away from us? They have taken our land, our families, our honor and dignity, our freedom. They even stripped my father of the only thing he had left of his heritage."

"What was that?" His wife's dark eyes questioned him as she tied her long, black hair into a knot.

"Just before the surrender to Nebuchadnezzar, Jehoiachin gave Abba the royal cloth that had been woven for King Solomon as a token of his right to the throne. When they pressed Abba into slavery, they stole it from him. Only God knows what they did with it. Abba talked about that cloth all the time."

Geula handed him a cup of fresh water. "I do remember him ranting on about some sort of cloth. I guess I never understood its significance. I miss his stories. I know he was entertaining the children, but his stories always touched my heart as well."

"He really believed we would someday return to the

Promised Land."

His wife placed a hand on his arm. "Keep your faith, Zerubbabel. God will not forsake His people. He has promised a Deliverer."

He let out a deep sigh. "I don't know how much longer I can wait for the Deliverer."

He sat in silence, the soft tones of his daughters' chatter fading as he lost himself in thought. He jolted when the door closed with a thud. His son stood with his back to the door, trembling like a pebble in the path of a stampede.

"Abiud, what's wrong? What's happened?"

"They stopped me, Abba. I was so afraid."

"Who stopped you?"

"The temple guards. I was on my way to Judah's house, but they stopped me and asked who I was. They asked what my occupation was. When they found out I didn't have one, they searched for me in their records and gave me this." The scroll he held out quivered in his shaky hand.

Zerubbabel grasped it, dread mounting as he unrolled it.

Abiud, son of Zerubbabel, captive of Babylon, is summoned for duty in the temple of Bel.

"I can't do it, Abba. I can't serve in their pagan

temple."

Chapter Eight

"Ezra, you have to help me. Surely you can influence the king to reassign my son to the palace."

His short friend shook his head. "It's more complicated than that, Zerubbabel. Their sacred festival is coming up. They need—fresh recruits."

"No, not my son. They don't need my son." He gripped his hair, pulling on it as if to make the anguish come from somewhere else. "There must be something we can do."

"The most powerful thing we can do is pray. We'll bring this up before the men tonight when we meet for prayer. You have a little bit of time. The boy will be cleansed for two weeks before he is actually put into service. In the meantime, keep him at home as long as you can."

*****

"Look at this, Abba. I carved a horse for Anna for her birthday."

Zerubbabel took the miniature carving in his hands. He ran his index finger along soft, smooth wood, admiring the delicate details. "Very well done. I think your little sister will be delighted."

Abiud's eyes, so like his mother's, sparked at the compliment. "I am making a new bread paddle for Imah too," he whispered.

A loud bang rattled the door. "Open up in the name of Bel."

Zerubbabel froze. What should he do? His wife came from the back room, their youngest clinging to her neck.

Another loud thud, and the door flew open. Temple soldiers swarmed the room, their spears and shields clinking with each swift step. Two stationed themselves on either side of him, ready to act if he attempted to resist. The commander came last, striding to the center of the room. He surveyed each of them — Geula, the children, Zerubbabel. Then he pointed at Abiud.

"That's the one. Take him."

Geula clutched the commander's arm. "No, please

don't take my son. I need him here. I have two small children. Please, let him stay."

"Your family has been honored this day, slave. Your son has been chosen to serve the great Bel." He shook loose of her grasp. "Consider yourself fortunate."

The soldiers seized Abiud by the arms. "Let go of me!"

They lifted his small frame, and his legs swung fast and hard. Abiud's foot caught one in the shin. Had it not been for the dozen other soldiers in the room, he might have escaped. A spear nicked his throat.

"Another move, and you'll serve as a dead sacrifice," the captain growled.

Abiud's eyes caught his, and the look of terror branded Zerubbabel's heart. As they dragged his son from the house, his carved horse fell to the ground and splintered into countless pieces.

*****

Word of Abiud's detention spread rapidly through the Jewish community. Many joined in fasting and prayers of intercession on his behalf, eating nothing, drinking nothing but water for more than a week. Zerubbabel spent hours in discussion with Ezra and Nehemiah, and even more hours in earnest prayer. Almost two weeks passed, still none of the schemes they concocted succeeded in convincing the pagan priest. Each time their pleas were rejected with an indifferent sniff and upturning of the nose.

His tired eyes drooped as he sat at the table. If his head didn't thunder in pain, and if his ears would cease their squealing, perhaps he could think. Or at least pray once more.

Geula approached holding a bowl of soup. With a gentle hand, she touched Zerubbabel's shoulder. "You must eat something, my husband."

He stared at the wooden bowl. Garlicky steam rose. His stomach rumbled, but he held up a hand and shook his head. "The two weeks have almost passed. Any day our son will be taken to serve in that terrible, dark pyramid."

His hand trembled as he nudged Geula away.

She sank to her knees beside him, still offering the bowl. "You are so weak.... You must eat. Starving yourself will not change the priest's mind. Surely, by now the Lord God has seen your fasting —"

"He is our son, Geula. A Hebrew. I cannot give up." He stumbled to his feet. The room spun, and in his haste to reach the door, he knocked over the wooden bowl, sloshing the potent liquid across the floor.

Geula rocked back and forth, arms hugged around her stomach. "I cannot lose both of you, Zerubbabel."

Turning away from her, he strode out the door. She was right. His fasting was not enough. Winding through the streets, pausing every other minute to take deep breaths and regain his balance, he finally reached Ezra's door. He rapped three times and slumped against the wooden frame.

The door opened, and Ezra's head poked out. "Zerubbabel?" The hinges groaned as he widened the opening. "Are you all right?"

"Our time is almost up. We have tried everything, yet none of it can change the heart of the priest. We have only one hope. To go to Cyrus the king and plead our case before him." He straightened and looked down at his small friend. "Ezra, you are a scribe, can you help me get into the palace?"

Ezra took a deep breath. "It isn't going to be an easy thing, my friend."

"I know. But it's the only choice we have."

Ezra's shoulders slumped, but he stepped into the street closing the door behind him. "Come with me."

Dodging chariots and cohorts of soldiers, Zerubbabel followed Ezra through the city streets. They passed under the arch honoring King Cyrus's conquests and wove through lush gardens of shrubs, flowers, and pomegranate trees. At last, they reached the citadel. Zerubbabel's thoughts raced like the Euphrates river beyond the gray stone walls. Their sandals thudded against the multicolored tiles as they approached the bronze gate leading to Cyrus's hall.

Ezra approached the man at the gate and bowed his head. "Ezra the scribe requests an audience with the king."

The man frowned, flicking the golden trim dangling from his turban back into place. "King Cyrus's schedule is full today. Come back later."

"Please, it is an urgent request regarding the recent acquisitions for the temple."

"Acquisitions?"

"Of persons, sir. For the ceremonies. I fear there may be a terrible mistake that requires the king's most urgent attention."

The gatekeeper pulled a scroll from his jeweled belt and scowled at it. "Not likely, but I will ask the king if he will make time for you, scribe."

"Many thanks." Ezra bowed and backed a short distance away.

The bronze door opened just enough for the gatekeeper to slip through, then closed again.

"If Cyrus grants me an audience, I will go in first," Ezra leaned close and whispered. "After I have introduced you and your relation to me, I will summon you, and you can make your plea."

Grating hinges sent shivers down Zerubbabel's spine. The gatekeeper's hand waved. "Enter, scribe."

Ezra patted Zerubbabel's shoulder before vanishing beyond the door.

Zerubbabel turned and paced, counting the green tiles as he stepped over them. He walked in circles, not wishing to stray far from the hall entrance. Would Ezra succeed in gaining the king's ear? Of all the plights the king heard in a day…

But what if he did? Zerubbabel's nerves tingled, and the hair on the back of his neck stood on end.

Lord God, give me the words to say. Grant me favor in the eyes of the king.

"My friend," Ezra's voice jolted him from his thoughts. "It's time. Are you ready?"

With a nod, he followed the scribe inside. He stared at his worn sandals as they crossed the green marbled floors. Finally, he found the courage to lift his gaze. The ceilings seemed as high as the stars, reminding him of his insignificance. Ivory stairs climbed past golden statues of elephants and lions leading to a matching throne.

Zerubbabel's long robe concealed his unsteady knees, but his hands betrayed his fear. He hid them behind his back as he approached the king. When his eyes reached the conquering monarch perched on cushions of lion skins, the last of his courage scurried away like the mouse burrowing beneath the fur rug.

"Kind and compassionate king, my friend is ready to make his request." Ezra backed out of the way.

King Cyrus's black eyes settled on Zerubbabel. He bowed his head in reverence, hoping to gain a moment to formulate an appropriate speech.

"Live forever, great majesty." His words came out hoarse. Clearing his throat, he sent up a desperate prayer begging the Lord to help him speak.

"Say on." The king folded thick arms across the giant jewel of his breastplate.

Zerubbabel's heart pounded so loud, he could barely hear his own words. "Majesty, my family and I have been devoted servants to the crown for many years. We have given our utmost to the king, serving him with vigor and performing our duties to the best of our ability. Your servant now has just one request."

The king's chin lifted, the heavy crown of gold and rubies gleaming from atop his head. "And what is your request, slave?"

Glancing around the room, Zerubbabel spotted Nehemiah who gave him a reassuring smile. Zerubbabel stepped closer. "I have one son, my lord, and two small children. My request, O king, if you would be so merciful, is that you would allow my son to work in the palace, in service to the king, rather than in the temple of Bel that he could be with his family and help my wife with the young children."

Cyrus frowned. "It is counted an honor to be chosen for the service of Bel. Why would you request his release?"

"Lord king, your servant is from a far off land. We do not worship the god of Bel."

"Then what god do you worship?"

"We worship the One True God of Israel who brought our fathers out of Egypt with a strong hand. The God of my fathers, David and Solomon, who made us a great and mighty nation. The God of Daniel, the wise councilor. The only living God, my lord."

"I have heard of this 'living God', as Daniel calls him. He tells me my bronze statues have no power."

Zerubbabel opened his mouth, but shut it just as quickly. What could he say? To offend the king could cost him his life, but failing to tell the truth... was worse. "Daniel is a wise councilor. I would not so exalt myself to challenge his wisdom."

Cyrus leaned forward, his eyes narrowing. "Who are you?"

"I am Zerubbabel, a servant in the house of my lord the king. It is my duty to polish the gold in the king's palace."

"What family do you come from?"

What family! He dare not tell the king he was of the royal line. Cyrus may have him killed in fear that he would conspire against him. But the king had left him no escape. "I am the son of Salathiel, the son of Jehoiachin whom Nebuchadnezzar carried away from Jerusalem."

The king grunted. "The grandson of the king of Israel shines my gold. It seems your living God has taught you humility."

"It seems impossible to teach a king's son to be humble, but our God specializes in the impossible, my lord."

"Well, son of Jehoiachin, it seems that your God may be bringing about the impossible again."

Zerubbabel's already weak knees nearly bent beneath him. Had he heard right? He had to know. "The king will spare my son?"

Cyrus chuckled. "I will do better than that. I like you Jews. You have convinced me your God is real." The king stood and descended from his gilded throne. "I have it in my heart to help you rebuild your temple in Jerusalem. Perhaps your God will then bless me as he blessed Nebuchadnezzar."[21]

A wave of shock vibrated through Zerubbabel. As his mouth slid open, the king grinned and clapped him on the shoulder. "Don't look so surprised. Didn't you just tell me of the power of your God? Now, as for your son, if you are who you say you are, and you are a son of David, then I will make you the governor of Jerusalem. In which case, your son must go with you. Your family, together with Ezra, will oversee the rebuilding of the temple."

"Th-Thank you, lord king." He could manage no more.

"You and Ezra will go through the house of the gods and sort out all the vessels taken from your temple. These will return with you to Jerusalem."

Ezra spoke up. "This is a great task and will take many people, my lord."

"Then take down this decree and issue it forth to all your people in Babylon."

Thus saith Cyrus king of Persia, The LORD God of heaven has given me all the kingdoms of the earth. Now, He has placed it upon me to build Him a house at Jerusalem, which is in Judah.

---

[21] 2 Chron 36:22-23

Who is there among you, of all His people, whose God be
with him? As many as will, let him go up to Jerusalem, and
build the house of the LORD *God of Israel, the living God, which*
is in Jerusalem.

And whosoever will not go, let them help by giving gifts of
silver, gold, goods, or beasts, as a freewill offering for the house
of God that is in Jerusalem.

The scribes made copies of the decree, and Zerubbabel
cradled one in his arm as he left the court. He hurried out
of the palace and veered into the nearest alley. He felt as if
his heart would burst. Tears of joy streamed down cheeks
that were growing tired, but he couldn't stop smiling. He
set the decree down on a barrel and stared at it. Shifting its
position once, then twice to view it from different angles.
Then he unrolled it and stared at the script. The moment
he let go, it rolled shut. Clenching his fists, he moved his
feet and hands together in an odd type of dance and
whirled around.

When his spinning ceased, he looked up to see Ezra
watching him. "I feel happy enough to dance too." Ezra
laughed. "Come. Let's tell the news near and far. The Lord
God has heard our prayers and given us favor in the sight
of our enemies."

Ezra turned and trotted toward the Jewish quarter.
Zerubbabel followed, quickening his step to catch up, but

when he did, Ezra moved even faster, then faster. Suddenly two grown men were sprinting through the city streets. Ezra gave a boyish whoop, and Zerubbabel couldn't help but join in. A head appeared in one of the shop windows—perhaps sporting a baffled expression—but he passed by so quickly he didn't have time to care.

When they reached the Jewish section, they split up and ran down each of the streets, rapping on every door they passed. All the while they shouted, "Hallelujah! Hallelujah! Deliverance has come!"

Men and women spilled into the streets, frowning at all the commotion. "Deliverance?" Each with a questioning brow followed them down the street. Ezra jumped up on the edge of the well, and the people gathered around him.

"What is this all about, Ezra?"

"Brothers, sisters, children of Israel, this day has the Lord God wrought wonders on behalf of His chosen. Adonai has heard our prayer, and your suffering is at an end!"

His exclamation was met with shrugs and baffled glances from one to another.

"Here." Zerubbabel raised the scroll above his head. "Is a decree from Cyrus. Listen, and you will hear words that the Almighty has placed in the heart of the king of

Babylon."

He placed the scroll in Ezra's waiting hand. The scribe unrolled the parchment and read it aloud. As he read the last segment, Ezra had to scream above the shouts of joy. Women grabbed tambourines and pounded rhythms that made Zerubbabel's feet dance. The notion spread, and soon dancing filled the streets. Those too old to dance sat and cried tears of joy.

For too many years, they'd served in captivity and great sorrow. But today, deliverance had come.

Chapter Nine

"No wonder no one ever comes out of this temple. It's too much work to go up and down." Zerubbabel panted as he and Ezra mounted the ziggurat steps.

Ezra straightened his short frame and chuckled. "Yes, and we're going to have to get all of the temple vessels down from here."

Zerubbabel stopped and surveyed the steps. "There must be an easier way." Good excuse for a rest if nothing else. "We'll have enough people that we can place someone every couple of stairs and hand the items from one person to another until they reach the bottom."

"The risk of someone dropping them is too great. One slip and the vessel would tumble all the way down and end up ruined at the bottom."

"You're right. Perhaps a pulley system of some kind."

"Maybe they have a hidden entrance with a more workable access."

Looking up at the stairs they still had left to climb, Zerubbabel huffed. "If there is such an entrance, I wish they would have told us before we started this climb."

When they reached the top of the ziggurat, Zerubbabel felt as if he'd reached the pinnacle of the world. Far below, horses and chariots raced through streets leading to the other temples and the citadel. Beyond, the river Euphrates adorned the city like a sapphire belt. Awe seeped into every fiber of his being. Few people saw this view, and he was here not to be imprisoned in the pyramid, not to become a sacrifice, but to carry away the treasures inside it. He felt like a thief…except he possessed the edict with permission.

Ezra presented the edict to the guard at the door. The man raised his bushy eyebrows as he read the content and glanced from them, to the scroll, and back again. He inspected the king's seal, then reluctantly returned the scroll and opened the door.

They entered a long corridor, the door shutting behind them. Darkness spread like a blanket, and heaviness settled over them. The air was close, and an odd smell permeated the place. They stood still, waiting for their eyes to adjust. But there was no light for their eyes to adjust to.

"Who enters the sacred temple of Bel?" The ghostlike voice made Zerubbabel jump. He bumped into Ezra, who must have taken it as a signal to speak up.

"I am Ezra, the scribe. I carry an edict from the king."

"Come forward."

So dark.... Nothing could be seen. Zerubbabel took one cautious step forward. He prayed for protection and took another step, then another, then another. His foot touched something. More stairs. He mounted one, two, three, four. Then there was light. A vast cavern surrounded him. Images of Bel encompassed the walls. At the back of the room rose a type of throne. A woman, clad in a colorful robe with three circular designs, reclined there. Insipid skin spread across her angular face, and she peered at them with jaundiced yellow eyes. Big dark pupils glowed at their center—like a reptile. A tall crown rested upon her head.

"Where is the edict you carry?" The priestess narrowed her eyes.

Ezra hesitated, but shuffled forward and handed over the scroll. Her eyes skimmed the lines, and her fist clenched and unclenched as she dug her long fingernails into her palms. She stood, shoving the edict back at Ezra.

"Follow me," the priestess hissed. "You may look, but you will take nothing from the treasury until I speak with King Cyrus."

She led them down stairs and twisting, turning corridors. Weapons of all sorts lined the walls. "At their spring festival, the Babylonians believe Bel fights a battle with many other gods inside this ziggurat. The weapons are for him," Ezra whispered.

Zerubbabel nodded. Their traditions mystified him. At least Ezra was here to explain, so he didn't feel lost in this foreign world.

"I take down many of the instructions for the festival every spring." Ezra gestured toward the woman leading them. "The king takes the high priestess as his wife during the festival."

Pity washed over him. How sad that King Cyrus would have to marry that creature in the name of a god of stone. Perhaps he would see the truth of Yahweh and put aside this pagan tradition.

At last, at the end of a long corridor, the priestess's torch gleamed off a door overlaid with gold and etched with an image of Bel conquering the dragon. She reached into her crown and produced a large key. She inserted it into the lock, turning it counterclockwise. It clicked several times before she slid the door to the left, revealing a silver door behind it, which she also unlocked using the key. After two more doors of bronze and iron, an opening appeared within a very odd doorframe, half clay, half iron. It reminded him of the dream Daniel interpreted for Nebuchadnezzar.

A stone hallway led to a cavern with a rounded roof painted like the night sky. Stained glass depicted the moon and stars. Fire burning inside gave them a glow. The colors cascaded onto the floor. Chests, tables, and hutches overflowed with treasures stolen from faraway lands.

"The spoils of Israel are in this corner." The priestess emphasized the word *spoils* as she waved her arm toward one pile.

Zerubbabel stifled a gasp. A corresponding thrill surged through his soul. Sure enough, the beautiful menorah, the basins, fleshhooks, tapestries, ephods, and breastplates for the priests. The brazen shields made by King Rehoboam. It was all there—everything his father described. Zerubbabel picked up a medallion and blew off the dust.[22]

"This scroll contains the account of what was carried away from the temple. You will find nothing missing." The priestess shoved the scroll at Ezra, spun on her heels, and stalked out of the room. "I will send a guard to make

[22] Ezra 1:7-11

sure you Jews don't take anything until I speak with Cyrus."

The heavy doors closed behind her, and the giant key clattered as it slid in the lock. They were locked in the treasury, just the two of them, with all the treasures taken from their precious temple. Zerubbabel stared at Ezra, then the treasure, then at Ezra again. His friend threw his arms around him and gave him a tight squeeze.

"Zerubbabel, did you ever think this day would really come?" Ezra laughed as he shook his head.

"To the Babylonians, this is just gold, silver, and bronze. But to us, it is so much more valuable than that. No. I didn't think I would ever see this day." Still holding the medallion in his hand, he traced the inscription of the menorah with his finger. A tear splashed onto the relic. In a mirrored movement, he and Ezra both swiped at their eyes. They laughed until the sound echoed through the chamber and they wept tears of joy. Then the great doors moaned open.

Their eyes were still wet when a guard approached. He looked from one to the other. "I've been sent to help you number the vessels. The king has authorized you to take only the things needed for the temple in Jerusalem."

Zerubbabel patted the man's shoulder. "We'll be glad for your help. The temple vessels are numerous, and we want an accurate count. What is your name?"

"Zardan. I have been a guard of this temple for over fifteen years, and they have never allowed foreigners in here. I don't know what you've done to win the king's favor, but you certainly have." The guard tipped his head to one side, casting pale skin and yellowed eyes into profile.

"It is not us, but our God who has granted us favor," Zerubbabel replied.

"I have also been instructed to tell you that the young man Abiud has been released from duty in the temple and sent home."

"Blessed be the Lord God of our fathers who has showed us great mercy and redeemed us from the hand of our enemies! Thank you, Zardan. That news brings great relief to me."

Zardan shrugged. "Should we start with the lavers?"

Ezra set up his quills and parchment. "Give me the count, and I will write it down and compare it to the numbers in the Babylonian chronicle. We'll then present it to the treasurer."

They sorted through the vessels for hours, separating the items into more accessible piles. Ezra made a mark on his scrip for each item, comparing the descriptions to those in the Babylonian scroll.

"I've been in this room many times to add to the collection of treasures from all over the world. We've moved your vessels three or four times to make more room for everything else." Zardan carefully unwrapped a piece. "Another fleshhook, Ezra."

"Do you know what those chests contain?" Zerubbabel pointed to a stack of wooden boxes against the wall.

"No, we never opened them, only moved them around."

Stepping over and in between golden bowls, he made his way toward the trunks. The stiff latch strained his thumbs. Then it clinked, and he lifted the lid. Purple, blue, and scarlet silks were folded in neat triangles. "Silks and tapestries in this one, Ezra. It looks like the tablecloths, hangings for the sanctuary, and…" A flash of color surfaced as he dug through the trunk. With both hands, he pushed back the other fabrics seeking the source. Under a fold of indigo, he found it. A fabric of seven colors woven together, with a six-point, long-tailed star at its center.

"Zerubbabel? What is it?"

He couldn't form the words to answer. Could this be what he thought? What his father had spoken of all those years?

Ezra brushed his arm as he peered into the trunk.

"That's nice. I don't remember it listed as part of the temple textiles."

"No, it was my father's. They took it from him when he reached Babylon. I can't believe it's here."

He gazed at Ezra, who couldn't possibly understand the value of the cloth. "These are the swaddling clothes of King Solomon. This is the heritage of the kings of Judah."

Ezra's eyes widened. "The Swa…? Unbelievable."

"I never expected to hold this in my hands. Ezra, Adonai truly is with us."

*****

Shofars blew as hundreds of Jews assembled in the street of Babylon, preparing for the journey to Jerusalem. Donkeys brayed, camels moaned, and Abiud chattered with his peers, waving his arms in dramatic motions.

Zerubbabel and Abiud had just finished loading their few belongings on a camel when Ezra appeared, his stocky body quivering with excitement. "Zerubbabel, the people are ready for their exodus."

"As am I. Abiud, hand me that spear, please." Reaching into the pouch at his side, he pulled out the swaddling cloth and tied it to the spear. "This, my friend, will be our banner of victory. The heritage of Judah once again returning to our homeland."

Handing the banner to his son, he climbed up next to a statue so all the people could see him. "People of Israel, this day the Lord our God has delivered us out of the land of our captivity. This day He has shown you that He is our Jehovah-Nissi, He is our banner!"

Then holding the banner high above his head, waving it like a symbol of triumph, he led their march out of Babylon toward Jerusalem. His parents had named him Zerubbabel, meaning "a stranger in Babylon", but he was that no longer. He was on his way to their homeland, with all the temple treasures, to restore the temple of the Living God.

*****

Circa 70 B.C.

Osnat opened an old wooden chest at the end of the bed and rummaged through it. "Your father had so many things. What did an old man need all this stuff for?"

Her husband's eyes grew misty. "Abba never threw anything out. The only way he ever parted with something is if he gave it to someone even less fortunate than ourselves. It's so hard to believe he's gone."

She placed a hand on his arm. "He is in the bosom of

Abraham, husband. He feels no more pain."

He nodded, so she went back to the chest. "Eleazar, do you know what this is?"

She held up a fabric with seven vibrant colors and a six-point star. Though pilled and faded, the fabric remained soft and pretty.

Eleazar frowned. "No, I don't remember ever seeing it."

"I wonder why he kept it."

"Perhaps my imah or savta made it? I don't know."

Shrugging, she placed it in a pile with the other linens. "I guess I'll keep it as a spare cloth, unless you want it for something?"

"Oh, look, his tallit." He reached for the blue and white shawl. "My abba was a man of prayer."

Leaving her husband to reminisce, she carried the pile of linens to the storage room.

Part Three

Chapter Ten

Circa 4 B.C.

The evening sun waned as Mary made her way to the well. The women of her small village glared at her as she approached.

"How dare she come to the well during the evening?" said one.

"Yes, Mary, in case you haven't heard, ill-famed women are to get their water during the day." The other woman sneered. "It isn't proper that the virgins should have to mix with the likes of you."

Their words stung, but Mary didn't answer. She

couldn't expect them to believe her claim. She had scarcely believed it herself. But when the words of the angel became manifest, she could neither doubt, nor deny it.

Setting the water pot on the mouth of the well, she touched her bulging belly. Girls had dreamed for centuries about carrying the Messiah. She had even heard of a daughter of a Pharisee who refused to marry, claiming that the Lord would choose her to bear the Deliverer.

Deliverer. They needed one now. The Jews had indeed returned to their homeland, but were still captives of gentiles. The iron hand of Roman rule embittered her countrymen.

"Can you believe she would ask her family to accept her story about an angel and that the life she carries is the Messiah? The daughter of a poor farmer?" The woman clicked her tongue. "That's dangerously close to blasphemy if you ask me."

Exhausted from the long walk to the well, Mary eyed the sycamore tree. How many times had she settled beneath its shade? But she didn't dare rest in the presence of these women. After filling her pot, she turned and waddled back toward home.

The thunder of hooves reverberated the ground beneath her feet. The only horses in Nazareth were Roman. Her heart pounded as she whirled around.

Approaching in a cloud of dust came a cohort of soldiers. Weeds tore at her ankles as she scrambled away from the road. She was hardly an arm's length away as the detachment passed without slowing. She closed her eyes, waiting for the sand to settle. Coughing grit from her lungs, she continued on her way.

Her feet and back ached by the time she crossed the threshold of Joseph's house. Had it really been three months since he brought her to live with him here? A smile tugged at her lips as she poured a cup of water. There were few men who would tolerate a pregnant woman with endless patience...especially one who carried a child that was not his. But Joseph did.

Grasping the cup of water, she slipped out into the sunlight and made her way to the shop behind their house. Joseph glanced up when she entered. "You look tired. Here, sit and rest awhile." He offered her the chair he had just finished for a rich man on the hill.

With a grateful smile, she handed him the cup and sat. "It's a fine and sturdy chair, Joseph."

His grin of satisfaction was so big, he could hardly sip the water. His dark eyes sparkled under his thick brows.

"A dispatch of Romans passed me on the road." She leaned back and scratched her stomach.

Joseph grimaced. "I wonder what they wanted."

"Probably more taxes."

He grunted and braced against his worktable. "They can't seem to tax us enough." He ran the back of his hand along his beard, as he did when he contemplated. "Maybe I should go see what it's about."

"I'd go with you, but walking to the well is enough for me these days."

"I wouldn't want you to go anyway. Safety is not where Romans are. I'll be back soon." He pulled on his outer coat.

Mary sat for several minutes after he had gone. It was good to rest, but there was much to be done. Lifting herself from the chair, she shuffled to the house.

She was grinding the flour for their evening bread when Joseph's heavy gait crossed the threshold. He stood in the doorway for a moment, stroking his beard.

"What is it? What did the soldiers want?"

"A decree from Caesar Augustus. Every man is to return to his own city, to be numbered and taxed."[23]

"To his own city? What does that mean?"

"It means I have to go to Bethlehem."

"Joseph, that's a three-day journey from here."

He nodded. "Yes. At least a week just traveling back and forth. And I don't know how long I'll have to stay in

[23] Luke 2:1-3

130

Bethlehem."

"The child will come during that time."

"Yes."

"I'm afraid to have the child without you here, Joseph. You know how the women of the village treat me. I don't know if the midwife will even help me."

"I'm sorry, Mary, but I don't have a choice. I have to go to Bethlehem." He stroked his beard again.

"Then I'll go with you."

"Impossible. Traveling can be treacherous, and you're far too close to the time. They couldn't have picked a worse time to travel. The spring weather is as predictable as an earthquake. It can be hot in the morning and storm fiercely in the evening. I can't have you going into labor on the side of the road with a storm moving in."

"You have family in Bethlehem?"

"Yes, uncles and cousins. My uncle, Manoach, owns an inn."

"Then we could stay there. The people of Bethlehem don't know us. They would only know me as your wife. They could not question the child."

Joseph folded his arms. "True. The situation in Bethlehem would be better for the birth. But traveling in your condition…"

"Yahweh will watch over His child. My place is with

you, as my husband. Where you go, I will go. Remember?"

His hold tender, he raised her hand to his lips, the only gesture of love he allowed between them. "You're a brave woman, and I love you for it. I will be glad to have you with me."

*****

The morning was warm and clear as Mary folded the last of the bread in clean napkins and tucked them into the bag. A long walk awaited them, and she prayed that the food she prepared would be enough. Hoisting the bag over her shoulder, she stepped outside.

When she peered inside the shop, there was no sign of her husband. Where would he have gone? "Joseph?"

A thud sounded from the far side of the room. "Ah!" Joseph backed out from under the table where he'd been working.

Mary bit her lip to keep from laughing. "Are you all right?"

He winced as he rubbed his head. "I think I'll escape death this time. Are you almost ready?"

"As long as I haven't forgotten anything. How are you going to leave the shop for so long?"

"Yigal has agreed to finish for me since he doesn't have to go anywhere. I think God created his family out of Nazareth dirt."

Mary laughed. "That's kind of him. I have prepared some bread for our journey. Do you think it will be enough?"

"What you have will do. Anything more we'll have to purchase along the way. I have just one more thing to do before we leave. Why don't you rest awhile? You'll need your strength for this journey."

"As you wish. Just tell me when you're ready."

Grateful for the rest, Mary laid down inside the house. She had closed her eyes, for what seemed mere seconds, when Joseph shook her.

"Mary, Mary, it's time to go."

Swiping the sleepy haze from her eyes, she sat up. Joseph helped her stand and led her outside. He tossed her bag on the back of a white donkey tied outside his shop.

She stopped. "What is that?"

Joseph looked up at her with a sparkle in his eye. "It's a donkey."

"Yes, but…how did you get it?"

"I traded for it. You didn't think I would let you walk all that way did you?"

"Oh, Joseph." She reached out and stroked the

donkey's neck. "What do you say, fella? Can you carry a heavy woman all the way to Bethlehem?"

Leaning to the donkey's level, Joseph imitated the donkey's bray. "Yeee-ssss."

Her abdomen cramped as she laughed at his impersonation.

"Come, let's be on our way." Giving her a broad grin, Joseph hoisted her onto the animal and grabbed its reins. The clip-clop of the mule's hooves on the cobblestones accompanied their procession through the village street. Nothing else. No friends calling out their goodbyes, no one handing them gifts and blessing their journey as they had when she had visited her cousin Elizabeth several months ago. How different now.

[24]Leaving Nazareth, they traveled down the Roman highway to Sychor, choosing the main roads as their safest route. They stayed with groups of other travelers whenever possible to discourage bandits.

Joseph insisted they travel slowly, for her sake, but that made for longer days. With no cities close by, they camped on the side of the road with another family also traveling because of the census.

The third day of travel seemed as if it would never end. Mary grew more and more uncomfortable, but tried

[24] Luke 2:4-5

not to shift too often and concern her husband. Dust caked his feet, and blisters formed on the back of his heels. She looked away.

Her mind drifted to the life forming inside her. The life the angel had said would be the promised Messiah. Emmanuel, God with us. What would it be like to raise a family with "God with us"?

"Joseph?"

"Hmm?"

"Are you nervous?"

His broad shoulders slumped. "I hoped you wouldn't notice. The family we camped with said they'd seen a family attacked by bandits on this portion of the road."

Mary pursed her lips. "What I meant was, about the child. If the Messiah is raised in our house, God will see our every sin."

"God already sees our sin, Mary."

"Yes, but what will it be like to have a child that…that…"

He faced her. "I know what you mean. I've been thinking about Him a lot too. Trying to remember all the prophecies. King David prophesied that the angels would bear Him up, that he wouldn't dash his foot against a stone. Maybe you won't have to kiss any skinned knees."[25]

[25] Psalm 91:12

Mary shook her head. "I don't understand why God chose us. The Messiah deserves so much more than we can give Him. Why would He come like this? To ordinary Nazarenes?"

"I suppose to prove that His love can reach that far."

Joseph tugged the reins, and the donkey started moving again. Several hours later, Jerusalem came into sight. High walls encompassed the city bustling with people. Through the arched Damascus gate, they entered a city more massive than anything Mary imagined. They passed the Roman fortress with its high towers and vigilant sentries, and then walked along the temple walls meticulously fashioned from enormous stones.

"I came here for the first time for my pilgrimage when I was thirteen," Joseph shouted over the noise of the crowds. "Ever since, we have come every year at Passover. That's a tradition I intend to carry on in our family."

"Jerusalem is amazing. I would like that. I would like to see inside the temple."

"You will get that chance, after the birth."

Mary's gaze flitted about…so much to observe, so many new things to see. They passed rows of tidy houses, lined up like soldiers. When they neared Zion gate, Joseph pointed to a beautiful palace.

"That is the palace of the high priest."

Early evening settled in by the time they passed Zion gate, the noise of the city fading behind them.

Mary's strength dwindled. Even keeping her balance on the donkey was difficult. She was ready to stop hours ago, but they had to reach Bethlehem tonight. "How much longer?"

"Bethlehem is still about five miles. I'm hoping we can make it before dark."

Five miles. She hoped she could hold on that long, but as the miles wore on at the donkey's slow pace, she grew nervous. Every once in a while, her stomach tightened. Beads of sweat trickled down her temples.

The cramping in her stomach worsened, and each time lasted a little longer. She soon became very uncomfortable.

Joseph glanced back at her. "Are you all right?"

"Yes, I'm fine," she said while holding her breath.

Her reply must not have convinced him, because he picked up the pace. "We'll be there soon."

She needed a distraction. "Joseph, will you recite the Torah for me? To make the time pass faster?"

"What passage should I recite?"

"I don't know, just something. Please."

"'Great is the LORD, and greatly to be praised in the city of our God. God is known in her palaces for a refuge. For, lo, the kings were assembled, they passed by together.

They saw it, and so they marveled; they were troubled, and hasted away. Fear took hold upon them there, and pain, as of a woman in travail.'"[26]

A contraction seized her, and she slumped over. "Not that one, something else."

"'My soul, wait thou only upon God; for my expectation is from him. He only is my rock and my salvation: he is my defense; I shall not be moved. In God is my salvation and my glory: the rock of my strength, and my refuge, is in God. Trust in him at all times; ye people, pour out your heart before him: God is a refuge for us.'"[27]

The contraction subsided, and Joseph urged the donkey to walk faster. The donkey's rapid gait lurched Mary from side to side. She gripped the mane to steady herself.

Another contraction. This time sending a surge of pain through her entire body. Gripping her stomach with one hand, and trying not to fall off the donkey with the other, she let out a fearful cry.

Joseph was instantly at her side, his eyes wide, his mouth gaping. "Mary, what is it? Are you all right?"

"The child—" she gasped between breaths. "He's

---

[26] Psalm 48:1-7

[27] Psalm 62:5-8

coming."

"Now? Can you hold on a little longer?"

"I don't know. I don't know."

Lunging for the reins, he jogged down the road, urging the donkey to match his pace. "Adonai, help us get there in time."

The sun was almost set when the little town came into sight. Mary groaned and clutched the donkey's mane, still she tilted too far to the right as they trotted downhill through another contraction. Her legs were too tired to give her much balance atop the beast, especially with the tightening of her stomach.

"My uncle's inn is just inside the gate."

Breathing deeply, Mary tried to smile at her husband's encouragement.

The town was brimming with travelers from all over the country, all blocking the arched entry to the village. Poor shepherds toted lambs on their shoulders, women wore weary scowls, and toddlers tugged on their parents' robes as tears streamed down their faces.

"Make way! Please, make way. My wife is in labor."

Mary caught a few curious glances before everything faded, and a firm hold gripped her abdomen. Perspiration caked her hair against her cheek.

Joseph knocked on a door. "Manoach, open the door!

We need a room, quickly."

No one answered. He pounded his fist against the door, rattling it upon its hinges. "Uncle Manoach, open to us!"

"We're full. There's no more room. Go somewhere else." An irritated voice came from an upper window.

Stepping backward, Joseph strained to see who answered. "Uncle Manoach?"

A white-haired man poked his head out of the window. "Who's there? Joseph?"

"Yes. Please, Uncle Manoach…my wife."

Another pain shot through her.

The front door flung open, and the man and a woman rushed out. "Joseph, I'm so sorry, but we're completely full. If only I'd known you were coming."

"Any room will do. Anything, please, the child is coming."

"Even our own room is full. We have moved all our children into one room with us to make room for travelers."

Mary grimaced at another pain.

Adonai, will you not provide for Your own child?

"Manoach, look at the poor girl. We have to do something," a feminine voice said.

Raising her head to the sky to catch her breath, Mary

noticed something strange. A star hung above the city, a star unlike any she'd seen before. Six rays of light spread out from its center, and the tail was longer than the other rays.

A piercing cry rose from her throat. It felt like she was in the grip of Satan himself. Her veil fell from her head as Joseph lifted her into his arms. Linking her hands behind his neck, she buried her face into his chest hoping to hide from the pain.

*****

"This way. I'm afraid it's all we can do."

Joseph carried his wife down the hillside behind the inn, careful of his step. Who had chosen to build this town on the side of a precipice? Below the house yawned the mouth of a small cave they had transformed into a stable.

Joseph stopped. A stable? He could not expect Mary to give birth in there. "Uncle, isn't there anything else?"

Manoach frowned and shook his head. "I'm terribly sorry, Joseph. Even all of our friends' houses are filled. Here you will at least have privacy."

I am entrusted with the woman who will bear God's son, and I can provide no more than this?

Mary writhed in his arms. "Joseph, hurry!"

His uncle penned all the animals at the far side of the barn as Joseph set his wife on a clean bed of straw. Sweat drenched her face, and her breathing shallowed.

"Hold on, my love. We'll call a midwife."

She gripped his arm. "There's no time. Joseph, you must help me. Don't leave me!"

The fear and pain in her eyes lanced his heart. He stroked her cheek to reassure her. "I'm here. I won't leave. I promise."

She relaxed and breathed a few times before pain again overtook her. A frantic feeling rose inside him as he looked around.

"I'll send Havalah with clean cloths and water." His uncle scurried away.

Adonai, is this how You will send Your Messiah?

Mary clutched his hand as her face contorted. In that moment, he felt helpless. He didn't know what to do. There was no one to help. His wife would bear her firstborn in a barn.

"Joseph, He's coming!"

"Now?"

"Now."

"What should I do?"

"Something!"

His heart thundered as he knelt before her.

"Ugh!" Mary's face contorted again.

A hand touched his shoulder. His aunt Havalah held out a bucket and a cloth. "Mop her face with a rag. This little one will be here any moment."

Relief flooded him as he crawled out of the way and doused the rag. With a gentle motion, he ran the cool rag across Mary's forehead. Her grateful eyes locked on his as she again gripped his hand. Then squeezing her eyes shut, she took a deep breath and gave one final push.

All was silent. Mary didn't breathe, didn't move. The babe didn't cry. His heart stopped beating. Blood saturated the cloths Havalah had brought.

His aunt gave the child two quick swats, and the precious wail of a newborn echoed off the cavern walls. Mary started to cry and reached for the child. Havalah deposited the babe into His mother's waiting arms, and she cradled Him close.

Awed, Joseph stood motionless as the babe quieted when she ran her finger along His cheek. "Jesus."

Taking the child, Havalah wiped Him clean with her last cloth. "Joseph, all these are soiled. Can you find something to wrap the babe in?"

He stood and glanced around the stable. What could he find? Mary's veil had disappeared, and their supplies remained by the inn.

"I'd brought out a spare cloth this morning to put beneath the cow's yoke. She gets terrible sores if we don't cushion it. The cloth should still be clean." Havalah pointed to the corner.

Draped over the ox yoke was a scrap of faded cloth. Picking it up, he brushed off bits of hay.

"Such a beautiful cloth. Look at all the colors." Mary smiled as he offered it to her. "It must have been lovely at one time."

His aunt tilted her head, her brow quizzical. "I don't know where it came from. It was in the linens my husband's parents gave to us."

"It is an odd piece. I think it has all seven colors. Is that a star at the center?" Joseph pointed at the yellow shape.

"It's perfect, as if it was made for us. The star looks like the one in the sky. Did you see it?" Mary's large brown eyes gazed up at him.

"A star?"

"Not just any star. It was different. It looked like that."

He stroked her hair. "You were in labor, my love. I didn't see any stars."

Spreading the cloth out in her lap, she laid the babe down. With her tender hand, Mary wrapped her firstborn son in the swaddling clothes.[28]

Picking up the soiled cloths, Havalah patted Mary on the arm. "I'll leave you to rest. I'll be back later to check on you."

Joseph knelt next to his wife and gazed upon the child in her arms. His face was calm, innocent. So this was the Messiah?

"Do you want to hold Him?"

"Me?"

Mary laughed. "You're the only other being with arms in this stable."

Joseph cleared his throat and lifted the babe from her arms. Tears welled in his eyes as he cradled Jesus in his bosom. He stroked the swaddling cloth.

"I'm so sorry it happened thus, Mary. I never imagined you'd have to give birth in a barn like an animal. And this is God's Son, wrapped in cloth meant for an ox. I don't understand why Yahweh would bring the Messiah this way."

Mary lifted an eyebrow and gave him a smile. "Perhaps, to prove that His love can reach this far."

The End

---

[28] Luke 2:6-7

Glossary and Pronunciation Guide

*Hebrew Pronunciation note: the 'ch' sound in most Hebrew words makes a sound like the "ch" in "Bach". It's a throat sound, and literally almost sounds like you're clearing your throat with almost a "Ha" sound. This sound will be symbolized by a star followed by a ch. (*ch)

Abba (Ah-bah)

Hebrew for 'father'.

Abishag (Ab-i-shag)

Young Shunnamite maiden summoned to serve King David in his late years. David's sickness caused him to not retain heat. A young virgin was sought from the kingdom to provide warmth for the aged king. Abishag was later requested by Adonijah to be his wife, however his request was not honored. Abishag is referenced in 1 Kings 1:1-4 & .

Absalom (Ab-sah-lom)

Third born son of King David. His mother Maacah was the daughter of Talmai the king of Geshur. Absalom conspired against his father and drove him out of Jerusalem, however, his reign was short lived and Absalom was killed by Joab, David's captain. References to Absalom can be found in 2 Sam 3:3, 2 Sam 13-19, 2 Sam 20:6, 1 Kings 1:6, 1 Kings 2:7, 1 Kings 2:28, 1 Chron. 3:2, 1 Chron 11:20-21.

Abiud (Ah-bee-odd)

Son of Zerubbabel, descendant of David and Solomon, ancestor to Joseph husband of Mary. See Matt 1:13.

Achbed (A*ch-bed) The 'ch' in this name is the Hebrew letter Haf. *See pronunciation note above.

Fictional assassin for Prince Absalom.

Adonai (Ah-d-oh-nie)

One of the Hebrew names for God, meaning Lord or Master.

Adonijah (Ah-d-oh-nie-jah)

Fourth born son of King David. Adonijah proclaims himself king after David is of old age and no longer healthy enough to rule. David counteracts his proclamation and makes Solomon king. Solomon spares his brother's life, but later Adonijah requests Abishag, the young maiden that tended his father, to be given to him to wife. This apparently political move angers Solomon who then has Adonijah executed by his captain Benaiah. Referenced in 2 Sam 3:4, 1 Kings 1&2, 1 Chron. 3:2.

Ahithophel (Ah-hit-o-fel)

David's aide and trusted councilor. Ahithophel is referred to in 2 Sam 15-17, 1 Chron. 27:33-34

Amnon (Ay-mon)

Eldest son of King David of Ahinoam the Jezreelitess. Amnon had a wicked heart and fell in love with Tamar, Absalom's sister. After feigning sickness , Amnon 'forces' Tamar and throws her out of his house. He was killed by Absalom's command. Amnon is referenced in 2 Sam. 3:2, 2 Sam. 13, and 1 Chron. 3:1.

Bathsheba (Bah-t-she-va)

David's fourth wife, and mother of Solomon. Bathsheba was the wife of Uriah the Hittite whom David had killed so that he could have Bathsheba as his own. The prophet Nathan rebuked David for his evil deed and cursed the child of their union, and the child died. God was moved by David's repentant heart which is expressed in Psalm 51. Bathsheba is referred to in 2 Sam. 11, 2 Sam 12:24, and 1 Kings 1 & 2.

Bel

Also known as Marduk, Bel is the main god of the Babylonian religion.

Benaiah (Ben-ay-uh)

One of David's mighty men, and later Solomon's captain of the guard. Referenced in 2 Sam 8:18, 2 Sam. 20:23, 2 Sam. 23:20-22, 1 Kings 1 & 2, 1 Kings 4:4, 1 Chron. 11:22, 1 Chron. 18:17, 1 Chron. 27.

Caleb (Kay-leb)

Fictional servant of Eliab, King David's brother.

Cyrus (Sy-rus)

King of Babylon and Persia around 559 B.C. Also known as Cyrus the Great, he issued a decree for the Jews to return to Jerusalem and rebuild the temple. He allowed Ezra and Zerubbabel to take the temple treasures back to Jerusalem for service in the new temple. Referenced in 2 Chron. 36:22-23, Ezra 1:1-8, Ezra 3:7, Ezra 4:5, Ezra 5:13-17, Ezra 6:3 & 14, Isaiah 44:28, Isaiah 45, Daniel 1:21, Daniel 6:28, and Daniel 10:1.

Eleazar (El-ee-ay-zar)

Decsendant of David, ancestor of Joseph, Mary's husband. He is mentioned in the lineage of Christ in Matt. 1:15.

Eliab (Ee-lie-ab)

Eldest brother of King David. See 1 Sam 16:6, 1 Sam. 17:13, 1 Sam. 17:28, 1 Chron. 2:13, and 2 Chron. 11:18

Elohim (El-lo-heem)

Hebrew word for God meaning "Creator" or "Judge".

El Shaddai (El-Sha-die)

Hebrew name for God meaning 'All Sufficient'

Ezra (Ez-rah)

Scribe, author of the book of Ezra in the Bible.

Ezra was commissioned by King Cyrus of Persia to oversee the rebuilding of the temple in Jerusalem. See the book of Ezra for his entire story.

Guela (Goo-lah)

Fictional name for the wife of Zerubbabel. Her actual name is not mentioned in the Scriptures.

Havalah (Ha-va-lah)

Fictional aunt of Joseph, Mary's husband.

Haggith (Hag-ith)

Wife of King David, mother of Adonijah. She is referenced in 2 Sam 3:4, 1 Kings 1:5 & 11, 1 Kings 2:13, 1 Chron. 3:2

Imah (Ee-mah)

Hebrew for 'mother'.

Jehoiachin (Je-hoe-a-kin)

King of Judah around 607 B.C. also known as Jeconiah. Descendant of King Solomon. Jehoiachin upset Nebuchadnezzar by refusing to pay the tribute in expectation that the king of Egypt would attack the Babylonian army. Nebuchadnezzar besieged Jerusalem and carried Jehoiachin and all the royalty, as well as the treasures of the palace and temple away to Babylon. He then placed Jehoiachin's uncle Zedakiah as king in his stead. Jehoiachin is referenced in 2 Kings 24:6-8, 2 Kings 25:27, 2 Chron. 36:8-9, Jer. 52:31, Ez. 1:2 Esther 2:6.

Jehovah Jireh (Ye-ho-vah Yee-rey)

Hebrew name for God meaning "God will Provide."

Jehovah Nissi (Ye-ho-vah Nee-see)

Hebrew name for God meaning 'God is my banner'.

Maacah (May-cah)

Wife of King David, mother of Absalom and Tamar. Daughter of Talmai the king of Geshur. Referenced in 2 Sam. 3:3, 2 Sam. 10:6.

Menoah (Men-o-ah)

Fictional uncle of Joseph, husband of Mary.

Mazel Tov (Ma-zel Toe-v)

Hebrew phrase used to express congratulations, usually for a happy or significant occasion or event.

Nathan (Nay-than)

Prophet and seer during the days of King David. Nathan is the prophet to rebuke David for his sin in taking Bathsheba, the wife of Uriah the Hittite, and having her husband killed. Nathan is also the one to bring the news of Adonijah's self ascent to Bathsheba, then David's attention. There are many references to Nathan in the scriptures 2 Sam. 7, 2 Sam. 12, 1 Kings 1, 1 Chron. 17, 1 Chron. 29:29, 2 Chron. 9:29, 2 Chron. 29:25.

Nebuchadnezzar (Neb-you-kuh-nez-zer)

King of Babylon between 605-562 B.C. He besieged Jerusalem three times, carrying away captives and the treasures of the palace and temple. Referenced in 2 Kings 24 & 25, 1 Chron. 6:15, 2 Chron. 36, Ezra 1:7, Ezra 2:1, Ezra 5:12-14, Ezra 6:5, Neh. 7:6, Esther 2:6, Jer. 27:6-8, Jer. 27:20, Jer. 28:2-4, Jer. 28:11-14, Jer. 29:1-3, Jer. 34:1, Jer. 39:5 he is also referenced throughout the book of Daniel.

Nitzevet (Nit-za-vet)

Traditional name for King David's mother.

Nun of Hebron

Fictional weaver of the swaddling clothes.

Osnat (Os-nah-t)

Fictional name for the wife of Eleazar, a descendant of David and ancestor of Joseph, Mary's husband.

Salathiel (Sa-lah-thee-el)

Son of Jehoiachim, king of Judah. Biblical texts are unclear as to whether or not Salathiel was born in captivity in Babylon, or carried away with the others after the siege of Nebuchadnezzar. Salathiel is referred to in 1 Chron. 3:17, Matt. 1:12, Luke 3:27.

Shabbat Shalom (Shab-bot Sha-lom)

Hebrew greeting for the Sabbath. Literally "Peaceful Sabbath"

Shofar (Show-far)

A type of trumpet made of ram's horn.

Solomon (Saul-o-mon)

Son of King David and Bathsheba. He reigns after David and builds the Lord's temple in Jerusalem. He is the compiler of the book of Proverbs, and considered to be the wisest man that ever lived. The Bible contains many references to him. 2 Sam. 5:14, 2 Sam. 12:24, 1 Kings 1-14, 2 Kings 21:7, 2 Kings 23:13, 2 Kings 24:13, 2 Kings 25:16, 1 Chron. 3:5 & 10, 1 Chron. 6:10 & 32, 1 Chron. 14:14, 1 Chron. 18:8, 1 Chron. 22-29, 2 Chron. 1-13, 2 Chron. 30:26, 2 Chron. 33:7, 2 Chron. 35:4, Neh. 12:45, Neh. 13:16, Jer. 52:20, Matt 1:6-7, Matt 6:29, Matt 12:42, Luke 11:31, Luke 12:27, You can also read the Song of Solomon which was a love letter between him and his beloved.

Tallit (Ta-leet)

Hebrew prayer shawl used to cover the head of male worshipers during prayer and Torah reading.

Tamar (Tuh-mar)

Sister of Absalom, daughter of David and Maacah. See 2 Sam. 13, 1 Chron. 3:9,

Yahweh (Yah-way)

Hebrew name for God meaning "You are the Lord

Zadok (Zay-dok)

High Priest during King David's reign. Referenced in 2 Sam 8:17, 2 Sam 15, 2 Sam. 17:15, 2 Sam 18:19-27, 2 Sam 19:11, 2 Sam. 20:25, 1 Kings 1, 1 Kings 2:35, 1 Kings 4:4, 1 Chron. 15:11, 1 Chron. 16:39, 1 Chron. 18:16, 1 Chron.

24:6 & 31, 1 Chron. 29:22.

Zardan (Zar-dan)

Fictional temple guard who served in the Babylonian Ziggurat.

Zerubbabel (Ze-rub-ba-bel)

Son of Salathiel of the lineage of David and Solomon. Zerubbabel returned to Jerusalem with Ezra to rebuild the temple. His was made governor of Jerusalem by King Cyrus of Persia. He is referred to many times in the book of Ezra, Nehemiah, Haggai as well as in Zechariah chapter 4.

Thank you for reading! We hope you enjoyed the journey.

If you enjoyed The Swaddling Clothes, please consider leaving a review on Amazon, Goodreads and your favorite sites. Telling your friends about the book is the best compliment you can give to an author.

You can contact the author and keep up with her new releases by connecting with her on the following links

Facebook:

www.facebook.com/AuthorAmberSchamel

Twitter: @AmberSchamel

Pintrest: www.pintrest.com/AmberDSchamel

or on www.AmberSchamel.com

CPSIA information can be obtained
at www.ICGtesting.com
Printed in the USA
LVHW112138201122
733664LV00022B/341